Jen.

Thank you so much for your help with this.

HARD

Scott Hildreth

I'll forever remember how this came together with both of us in a mess over it.

You're great!

Scott :)

This book is a work of fiction. Names, characters, places, and incidents are the product of the author's imagination or are used fictitiously. Any resemblances to actual events, locales, or persons living or dead, are coincidental.

Copyright © 2016 by Scott Hildreth

All rights reserved. In accordance with the U.S. Copyright Act of 1976, the scanning, uploading, and electronic sharing of any part of this book without the permission of the author or publisher constitute unlawful piracy and theft of the author's intellectual property. If you would like to use the material from the book (other than for review purposes), prior written permission must be obtained by contacting the author at designconceptswichita@gmail.com. Thank you for your support of the author's rights.

Published by
Eralde Publishing

Cover model: Michael Wajchert

Photography by: Reggie Deanching @ R+M Photography

Cover Design Copyright © Creative Book Concepts
Text Copyright © Scott Hildreth
Formatting by Creative Book Concepts

ISBN 13: 978-1535196918
All Rights Reserved

DEDICATION

To the nameless woman who was raped, only to see her rapist receive six month's jail time.

This is not justice, but it is all I have.

And it is for you.

PROLOGUE

PEYTON

I pushed his office door open just enough to peer inside. He stood at the far side of his desk with his hands on his hips and his eyes fixed on the skyline. I cleared my throat. "Your email didn't make a lot of sense."

He turned to face me and shrugged. His crisp white shirt didn't have a single wrinkle in the fabric, a reminder of how early in the day it was. He studied me for a moment and shook his head lightly. "It was as straightforward as it could be."

It wasn't. It never was with him. His cryptic messages – always without punctuation – made it problematic to understand his desire, and even more difficult to believe he was the editor-in-chief of the Union-Tribune, San Diego's largest newspaper.

But he was. No differently than his father, and his father's father, Camden Rollins III was the man in charge.

I swept my thumb across the screen of my phone and stared at the email. "Need something on filthy fuckers make it hard edgy and in-your-face maybe a three or four installment piece depending on what you find."

He brushed his hands along the thighs of his pants, chuckled, and sat down. "Everything you need is right there." He motioned to the chair positioned in front of his desk. "Have a seat, Peyton."

HARD

I shoved my phone into the front pocket of my jeans, walked into his office, and sat down. "What – or who – are filthy fuckers?"

"You're not much of a reporter." He chuckled. "*The* Filthy Fuckers are an Outlaw Motorcycle Gang. But, like all the motorcycle gangs, they like to be called a *club*. You know, like the Sons of Anarchy," he said.

Tattooed men made me go all wobbly-legged. Tattooed *bikers* made my lady bits ache. I nodded eagerly. "I'm going to do a piece on a motorcycle club? A *real* motorcycle club?"

There were very few television personalities I cared for, but no differently than half of the female population in the nation, I'd crawl naked through a mile of broken glass for a chance to suck Charlie Hunnam's cock.

"Real? Yeah, these guys are real, alright. The Filthy Fuckers are as rough as it gets. President's name is Nicholas Navarro. He goes by Nick or *Crip* to his brothers in the club. You'll need to interview him personally unless you want rumors and bullshit. Scuttlebutt around town is that they're close to declaring war with Satan's Savages. After some of what we've seen from these clubs in the past, The Union-Trib would like to call it before it's national news."

"Holy shit. Yeah, I'm stoked," I said. "Not that I'm complaining, because I'm not, but if you don't mind me asking, why me? A girl doing a four installment piece of a motorcycle gang?"

"Three or four, depending on what you uncover." He leaned back in his chair, folded his arms in front of his chest, and shook his head. "And why you? You're a thrill-seeking weirdo, and everyone here knows it, including me. That's why. Half my staff would be scared to death, but you'll dive in head first."

He was right, except for the weirdo part. I loved driving my Jeep to the most remote place I could find, parking it, and rock climbing wherever I wasn't able to get to by vehicle. Hang gliding and paragliding from the cliffs at the Torrey Pines Gliderport in La Jolla was a common occurrence for me. And, I always volunteered to follow each unsolved death in the city, hoping I could turn it into a homicide, but so far it never happened.

"I'm not a weirdo," I said in a matter-of-fact tone.

"An adventurous reporter who leaves no stone unturned."

"I like that better," I said. "So what do I do? They're not just going to agree to talk to me."

"Do your research. You'll figure something out."

"That's it? That's your best advice?"

He leaned forward, adjusted his tie, and sighed. "When was the last time you did what I told you to do?"

I shrugged.

"Precisely. You're going to do what it is you do. So, go do it. Just make it interesting. We need something awe-inspiring."

I stood from my seat and nodded. "Awe-inspiring four installment piece, coming right up, Mr. Rollins."

"Three or four," he said. "Depends on what you find."

The thought of rubbing elbows with the members of a motorcycle club made me tingle all over. "You might not see me for a while. But, if it's out there," I said. "I'll find it."

"Take all the time you need," he said. "Just make sure three or four weeks is enough."

Three weeks with a real-life Jax Teller?

He had assigned me to three weeks in fucking heaven.

I turned toward the door. "See you in four weeks."

"Three or four," he snapped back.

Yeah, I guess it all depends on what this Navarro guy looks like.

"What's he look like? Navarro?" I asked over my shoulder.

"He's a big muscular fellow that's covered in tattoos from head to toe, including his hands. Likes to drink beer and fight. Rough dude. Like I said, do your research first."

Tattooed alpha male biker?

"See you in four weeks," I said with a laugh.

Maybe longer.

ONE

PEYTON

I walked along the row of motorcycles that were parked outside the bar. Some of them were apparently new – fitted with painted saddle bags and multi-speaker stereos, while others were older and adorned with nothing more than a solo seat, a leather tool pouch, and ape hanger handlebars.

Albeit short, my study of Harley-Davidsons – and the men who rode them – provided me with enough information that I found the motorcycles, the men, and the concept of a close-knit biker club fascinating.

I couldn't help but wonder what level of rejection I was going to get. There was no doubt in my mind that the members of the *Filthy Fuckers MC* weren't going to agree to sit down and answer all of my questions over a glass of beer.

Dressed in cut-off jean shorts, Chuck's, and my favorite tee shirt, I walked across the scorching asphalt parking lot toward the bar's entrance.

I reached for the door, inhaled a shallow breath, and pulled it open.

Just be yourself, Peyton.

I stepped into the poorly lit bar and realized the only patrons were bikers. I was met by no less than twenty-four eyes, two of which I immediately recognized.

HARD

Nicholas "Crip" Navarro was the president of the Filthy Fuckers MC, and despite my being fifteen years his junior, I found him to be extremely attractive. He was 42, covered in tattoos, and as handsome as any man I had ever seen. Him being a biker made him even more attractive.

While mentally preparing to infiltrate the club, I studied many photos of the club's known members, their motorcycles, and of Nick. In doing so, one thing stood out in each and every picture of him.

His remarkable blue eyes.

Now that they were locked on me, I searched for a glimmer of hope that I could remain strong-willed, independent, and above all, professional.

With my head held high, I clung to the thrill of the challenge, and walked directly toward the group of drunken bikers. Dressed in jeans, boots, and his leather vest, Navarro stood from the bar stool at his high-top table and turned to face me. With a bottle of beer dangling from one hand, he raked the fingers of his free hand through his black hair, brushing it away from his face.

His eyes fell to the floor and then slowly raised the length of my torso. After pausing to stare at my tits for a few long seconds, he eventually met my gaze. "You lost, little girl?"

I stutter-stepped, not quite knowing what to do. Roughly a dozen men surrounded him, and although they all looked at me with lustful eyes, it seemed they were waiting on his approval or rejection of me before they made any comments or passed judgement.

I swallowed hard and returned his stare. "No. I'd uhhm. I'd. I'd uhhm. I'd like to talk to you," I stammered.

His eyes dropped to my bare legs. He grinned, revealing teeth much whiter than I expected him to possess. He raised his bottle of beer, took a drink, then lowered his chin slightly. "Show me your tits," he demanded without so much as an ounce of expressed emotion.

Excuse me?

It wasn't at all what I expected. I cocked my hip. "Excuse me?"

He took another drink of beer and wiped his mouth with the back of his hand. "You want to talk to me? Show me your fuckin' tits."

Causing any other man to respect me would have required a *no* answer. To get Nick Navarro to respect me meant I needed to bare my tits.

I cleared my throat.

Twice.

I nodded toward his waist. "Show me your cock."

The man at his side, a muscular giant with collar-length hair and an awesome full beard, choked on the beer he was in the middle of swallowing and coughed out a laugh.

Navarro didn't so much as crack a smile. Still cradling the bottle of beer in his hand, he reached for his belt, unfastened the buckle, and struggled to push his faded jeans down his thighs. As the material cleared the base of his dick – revealing a few inches of the rather thick shaft – my eyes shot wide.

Holy shit.

I wondered just how far he would go.

While I stood and waited, fairly certain he wouldn't get his *entire* cock out in a public bar – especially amidst the members of the MC – he pushed the denim a little further and it sprung free.

Well, there's the answer.

I stood, open-mouthed, and did what any girl in the same situation would have done.

I stared.

I enjoyed the scenery for a few seconds less than I really wanted to, laughed to myself at the thought of including the scene in my first written installment, and regretfully tore my eyes away from his thickness.

With the waist of his jeans at mid-thigh and his dick dangling from between his legs like the heavy slab of meat that it was, he raised the bottle of beer to his lips and took a drink no differently than if he was fully clothed.

I couldn't help but wonder why he didn't pull his jeans up, but was too wrapped up in the excitement of it all to give matters much serious thought. My heart felt like it was beating between my ears. I desperately wanted to take another look at his massive cock, but didn't dare turn the event into any more of a sexually frustrating situation than it already was.

With his eyes locked on me, he finished his beer, handed the empty bottle to the six-foot-ten giant, and pulled up his jeans. He fastened his belt and cocked an eyebrow slightly. "Get 'em out."

What the fuck have I got myself into?

I inhaled a breath of courage, glanced around the bar, and made note that there was no one present except for me and the bikers. No waitress, no bartender, no *nothing*. Although I shouldn't have, I found the thought of revealing my tits in front of the group of bikers to be sexually stimulating.

But, as my boss had clearly stated, I was a *thrill-seeking weirdo*.

Against my will – and best judgement – my pussy began to tingle.

I pulled my tee shirt over my head, shoved a portion of it into the back pocket of my shorts, and lowered the straps of my bra past the sides of my upper arms. While each and every wide-eyed biker stood in wait, I cradled the cups of my bra with my hands and pulled them down slightly, revealing the full 'C' cup boobs that made me the most sought after freshman in high school.

Navarro shook his head. His mouth twisted into a shitty little smirk. "Take off the bra."

A tingling ran the length of my body, from my neck to my calves and back. But, instead of rubbing my goose-bump covered arms, I unfastened my bra, pulled it forward, and tossed it toward the giant who was apparently Navarro's body guard.

Not that he needed one.

The bearded biker snatched my bra from the air in mid-flight. I made note of the patches on the front of his vest.

Pee Bee. Sergeant-At-Arms.

My focus shifted back to Navarro. His slight smile made me comfortable, and I quickly got lost admiring his eyes. I cocked my head to the side and pressed my biceps against the edges of my breasts. "Satisfied?"

He pursed his lips, stared at my tits for a few long seconds, and nodded. "Nice set of tits."

I did my best to offer him a curtsy. It probably looked like I lost my footing and stumbled.

His eyes narrowed. "So, who the fuck are you?"

I pressed my tongue to the roof of my mouth, fought to swallow, and reached for my shirt. "Peyton. Peyton Price."

"What'd you do, back your Hyundai into my fuckin' bike?"

His entire body was covered in ink. Even his neck and knuckles were tattooed. He was far better looking than I expected him to be. I pulled my shirt over my head, situated it, and shook my head. "No. I parked fifty feet from you guys. I wanted...I uhhm. I'm a reporter for the newspaper. The Union-Tribune. I'm doing an article, a three or four-piece installment on outlaw motorcycle gangs. I'd like to interview you."

He stepped so close I could feel his breath on my face. "No gang members here, we're a club," he breathed.

He smelled like a gasoline and adrenaline. My nostrils flared, my mouth watered, and my throat tightened. I swallowed heavily and muttered my response. "A uhhm. A club. An outlaw. An outlaw motorcycle *club*. Sorry, I misspoke."

It was a foolish mistake.

He leaned away and shot me a glare. "Well, reporter, you better get your shit straight before you go writin' anything. Some half-wit motherfucker goes and calls us a gang in the newspaper, and we'll all be doing time in the joint under the RICO act."

"So you'll agree to it?" I asked excitedly.

He inched closer, completely obstructing my view of everyone who surrounded him. He raised his clenched fist in front of my face, extended his middle finger, and widened his eyes.

I peered beyond his tattooed finger and widened mine in return.

With our eyes locked, he slowly lowered his hand. The lack of space between us made doing so rather difficult, and his tattooed bicep lightly brushed against the nipple of my left breast. I shuddered as a result, quickly reminded that I hadn't taken the time to get my bra back from his oversized body guard.

I felt the tip of his finger trace along the inside of my leg, just above my knee. Feeling his hand on my flesh did little to excite me. It was impossible.

I was already soaked.

Although I wanted desperately to look down and see just what it was he was doing, I kept my eyes fixed on his, rolled my shoulders slightly, and straightened my posture. He needed to know I wasn't just some dumb girl who was going to be scared away easily.

I've got news for you, Nick Navarro, you're not going to intimidate me.

The tip of his finger rose the length of my inner thigh for what seemed like a lifetime. He must have perceived the lack of objection on my part as an invitation to continue.

Still focused on his hypnotic eyes, I tried to refrain from showing any emotion. With him teasing me while a dozen of his brethren watched, it didn't come easily. His hand came to rest at the frayed opening of my shorts.

His mouth twisted into a smirk.

I tried to swallow, but didn't quite succeed.

I felt his finger slide beneath the leg of my shorts.

You're not going to...

As he circled my clit with his tattooed digit, I considered objecting to his little game, but the words never came. Had I protested, it would have been a lie. My boss was right, I was a thrill-seeking weirdo, and having an outlaw biker come close to fingering me at noon in a remote bar in Escondido, California stood as all the proof that was needed.

Without warning, he pushed his finger inside of me.

Completely.

I gulped a breath.

So much for remaining professional.

He stared into my eyes and grinned. "You like that, do you?"

I wasn't a whore. Hell, I wasn't even what a person that anyone in their right mind could describe as promiscuous. But, for whatever reason, I was allowing Nick Navarro to finger fuck me while the beer guzzling members of his *club* eagerly watched. Be it because I desperately wanted to write the piece, or because I found tattooed bikers insanely attractive was irrelevant.

The fact remained that the president of the Filthy Fuckers MC had his middle finger shoved so deep inside of me that I could feel the palm of his hand against my clit.

And, I liked it.

A lot.

He curled the tip of his finger against my g-spot a few more times, bringing me to a shallow climax. Guilt washed over me. I made a feeble effort to writhe away from him, but failed miserably.

He gripped my neck with his free hand. "Going somewhere?"

An inaudible *no* puffed from my lips.

He pushed his finger deep and held his hand still.

I exhaled against his tattooed neck.

"Be at our clubhouse tomorrow at six o'clock," he growled. "If you're worth a fuck as a reporter, you'll find it. Between now and then, I'll decide if I'll talk to you."

As he pulled his finger from inside of me, I considered the possibility of him *not* wanting to talk to me after I showed up at his clubhouse.

I tugged against the legs of my shorts in an effort to situate myself. It provided no comfort whatsoever. I was way past horny and my pussy was a sopping wet mess.

I had no intention of sticking around while the other members of the club ogled me or expressed how they thought less of me for allowing their president to finger me senseless in their presence. I decided to wear the finger-fucking experience as a badge of honor. "Thanks for the talent-fingers," I chimed. "I'll see you at the clubhouse tomorrow at six."

He grinned.

I grinned in return, turned away, and took a few steps toward the door. "For what it's worth," I said over my shoulder. "You've got a magnificent cock."

And your finger's not bad, either.

TWO

NICK

Pee Bee was the club's Sergeant-At-Arms. The enforcer. The position didn't require him to be organized, and maybe that was a good thing, because it seemed he often fell short in that respect. Based on his lack of planning alone, I often wondered why both of us weren't doing time in prison.

Serious time.

"What do you mean, you *hope* he's not home?"

It was midnight, and being dressed in black helped conceal us from the view of potential late night onlookers, but at six foot eight and 260 pounds, hiding Pee Bee entirely was like trying to cover up a circus elephant with a fucking cocktail napkin.

He turned to face me and shot me a confused stare. "It means I hope he's not home, Crip."

Positioned fifty feet behind the home we were planning on breaking into, I glared back at him. "After we crawled through a dozen back yards, waded through a fuckin' river in the storm sewer, then hiked three fuckin' miles you're not *sure* if this prick's gone?"

He pulled his backpack over his shoulders, removed a wire coat hanger, and shrugged. "Supposed to be at a wedding."

"Supposed to be?"

He nodded an unconvincing nod. "That's what I was told."

My service as a Navy SEAL made our late night theft of two motorcycles simplistic in comparison to some of the missions I had been involved with. It did very little, however, to assure me that we weren't going to be caught. "I hope your source was good."

He straightened the wire into a four-foot-long hook. After a quick inspection of his break-in tool, he shoved a wooden wedge into his pocket and then shouldered the backpack. "Yeah, me too."

Still positioned deep in the back yard, I watched the home for several long seconds. All of the windows were dark, and there were no flickering lights, which led me to believe no one was home watching television.

With slight reluctance, I decided to proceed. "Ready?"

He nodded. "Yep."

I pointed toward the corner of the house. "We'll go around the left side of the house, and I'll stay beside the garage until you're inside. After the door's up, I'll hop in there with ya. As soon as I do, pull the fucker closed until we get 'em unlocked."

He straightened the wire a little more, then held it at arm's length for an inspection. "Got it."

Breaking into a garage was easy. It took a coat hanger, someone with a steady hand, and less than ten seconds. The two motorcycles we were taking would be just as simple, requiring nothing more than a Bic pen to steal them.

After having a brother's bike stolen from a bar one Saturday night, stealing the president of Satan's Savages bikes in retribution was a risk I was willing to take. The president of most motorcycle clubs would demand that a prospect commit the theft as an initiation to the club.

But I wasn't a typical president.

I'd never ask my brothers to do anything I wasn't willing to do myself.

After cautiously walking around the front of the house, I stood watch while Pee Bee worked his magic. Five seconds later, and he quietly opened the garage door. After I ducked inside, he pulled the door down behind me.

The garage was empty short of the two motorcycles that were parked inside. "The Super Glide's unlocked," he said after reaching for the key switch.

I turned the key switch of the Softail. I wasn't as lucky. "This one's locked."

I reached in my pocket, pulled out a Bic pen, and pushed the barrel of the pen into the round key opening. After a few seconds, the lock turned freely. "Good to go," I said. "Open the door. We'll take Oceanside back toward the freeway and meet at the shop."

He grabbed the handle of the garage door. "Sounds good."

I raised my leg over the seat, sat down, and started rolling the motorcycle toward the closed garage door. The sight of the door leading into the house swinging open made the hair on the back of my neck stand up.

Someone shouted from just inside the house. "What in the fuck!?"

It wasn't the Savage's president, Whip, but the guy could have easily passed for his brother. I kept my eyes locked on him while trying to get off the bike, and soon decided it must have been Whip's brother.

"Motherfuckers," he grunted as he turned and ran inside the house.

Pee Bee's eyes met mine and instantly went wide. There was now a risk if we attempted to leave – the man inside the house may return with a gun before we got away. I realized the risks associated with breaking into the home, but I had zero desire to get shot in the back. With little time to think, and even less to react, I swept the kickstand down and steadied the bike.

Pee Bee shot past me and ran into the house after the retreating man.

It seemed like a fool's move, but it was probably our best bet. Without as much as a second's thought, I followed right behind him. As I rounded the corner to the living area, I heard the unmistakable sound of fists hitting flesh.

"What were you gonna do with that?" I heard Pee Bee shout. "You a fuckin' baseball player?"

With his legs in the living room, and his upper body concealed by the doorframe of what I suspected was the bedroom, Whip's look-alike was on his back. A baseball bat lay beside him on the floor, and Pee Bee sat on his chest, pounding him without mercy, one fist at a time.

As no one was coming to the beating victim's rescue, I immediately assumed the small home was empty – short of the guy getting pummeled by Pee Bee. My experience in the military, however, taught me that assumptions could get a man killed.

I quickly searched the home, found it empty, and walked back to the living room. When I returned, the man on the floor appeared to be unconscious, and Pee Bee still straddled him while digging through his backpack.

"Come on, let's beat feet," I said.

"Hold up," he responded.

He pulled a roll of duct tape from the bag. "This ought to work."

I chuckled. "For what?"

"Taping him up."

"What the fuck for?"

He stood up glared at me as if I were an idiot. "So the dumb fucker doesn't call the cops or whatever."

I nodded and stepped toward him. "Let's make it quick."

While I held the man's legs above the floor, he taped his ankles together with about a dozen wraps of tape. After tearing the tape in two, he then taped the man's arms to his torso with an equal amount of tape.

He swung the toe of his boot into the side of the man's head. "Pick up his head."

I laughed to myself and lifted his head from the floor by his neck. He began to moan; a sign he was obviously regaining consciousness.

Pee Bee kicked him in the side of the head again, hard.

"God damn." I chuckled.

"Fucker came at me with a ball bat, Crip. Fuck this dude."

"I'm with ya," I said. "Just make it quick."

From his forehead to his chin, he wrapped the man's head in duct tape, making it one solid ball of grey tape. It wasn't what I was expecting, but it would definitely be effective in keeping him from talking.

While Pee Bee placed the remaining portion of tape back into the backpack, the man started to thrash around. I realized in the rush that Pee Bee hadn't taken time to leave any air holes in his handiwork.

I motioned toward our flopping victim. "Fucker's suffocating."

Pee bee sighed. "How long's it take for a guy to, you know, run out of…" he paused and shouldered his backpack again.

"Oxygen?"

"Yeah," he said with a nod. "Oxygen."

"Maybe a minute or so?" I shrugged. "Something like that. Give or take."

The man continued to thrash about, flopping like his life depended on it.

"Maybe we ought to poke some breathing holes in that tape, huh?"

"Unless we're tryin' to kill him," I responded.

"Still got that pen?"

"Where's yours?"

He shrugged. "I dunno."

I pressed my hands to my pockets, realized I didn't have my pen, and then remembered it was still in the key switch of the Softail in the garage. "It's in the fuckin' garage. Be right back."

I sauntered to the garage, retrieved the pen, and returned. Pee Bee was standing over the man with his arms crossed, staring down at him.

He nodded toward the motionless man and shrugged. "He quit."

"Quit what?"

He pressed the sole of his boot into the man's hips, pushing him across the floor a few inches. "Moving."

"How long's it been?"

He narrowed his eyes and stared back at me. "How long's what been?"

I knelt down, poked two holes in the tape where I expected his nostrils to be, and waited. "Since he fuckin' moved."

He shrugged. "I dunno. Fucker was floppin' when you went to get the pen, then he just stopped."

I took his pulse.

Nothing.

I sighed. "Fucker's dead."

He returned a stare of disbelief. "Are you kiddin' me?"

"Nope." I shook my head and stood up. "Dead as fuck."

The plan was to steal the two motorcycles as payback for what Satan's Savages had done. I was a firm believer in an eye for an eye. A theft on their part deserved a theft in return. Murder wasn't out of the question, but it definitely wasn't something I had planned on when Stretch dropped us off.

I cleared my throat. "Gonna call Stretch and have him drive around to the block west of here. The way we came in. We're gonna toss this prick in the back of the truck and haul him to the shop."

"Why don't we just leave him here?"

"His dead ass is proof we committed murder. If we take him, it might be a couple of days before Whip calls it in, and even then, it'll just be a missing person report. See if you can find his cell phone, we'll take it, too. And we'll need to wipe this place down, anywhere and anything we touched."

"Got it."

"And we're leaving the bikes," I said.

"What the fuck for?" he snapped. "We need some get back for what these bastards did."

"If we take 'em now, it'll sure look to Whip like it was the work of the Fuckers. If we take the dead guy and leave the bikes, Whip ain't gonna suspect shit. And I think killin' Whip's brother is enough get back for stealin' a bike."

He nodded. "Good call."

I grabbed a hand towel from the bathroom and wiped down the bikes, door handles, the garage door, and the bathroom. After convincing ourselves the entire place was free of our fingerprints, I pocketed the dead man's cell phone and grabbed the baseball bat.

"Ain't no sense in draggin' his dumb ass. We'll get caught for sure,"

Pee Bee said. "I'll just carry the fucker."

We only had to go a hundred yards, but carrying a dead body wasn't as easy as one might think. My experiences in combat taught me that the dead and wounded were more difficult to carry than someone who was alive and well.

With minimal effort, Pee Bee hoisted the dead body over his shoulders. "Lead the way."

Using my shirt to keep from leaving fingerprints, I opened the back door. "Through this yard, then through that yard. Stretch is parked in the street. Ready?"

He nodded.

Without incident, we rushed through the two yards, and up to the side of Stretch's truck. I checked over each shoulder. "Toss him in the back."

"Open the door," Pee Bee demanded. "I'm puttin' him in front with us. It'll look like he's drunk."

"Toss his ass in the fuckin' back," I growled.

He shifted the dead body on his shoulders and glared back at me. "We get caught with him in the back, we're fucked. Open the fuckin' door."

"You two fuckers need to get in here, or we're all gonna get got," Stretch warned. "Hurry the fuck up."

"Toss his ass in the back," I demanded.

"Sure thing, *Boss*." He sighed, rolled his shoulders forward, and ducked his head. The dead body rolled over the top of him and dropped into the back of the truck with a thud. "We get busted, it's on you, Crip."

I pulled the truck door open and motioned toward the inside of the cab. "We ain't getting' busted, I'm sick of arguing about it. Get in the fuckin' truck."

After a short glare, he got in.

With the dead body in the bed of the truck, we rode to the shop in silence. Strangely, I wasn't concerned with murder charges, Whip's dead brother, or disposing of the body. My focus was elsewhere.

The girl from the bar with the tight little pussy and the mile-long attitude was on my mind, and as much as I didn't want to admit it, I was looking forward to seeing her again.

There probably wasn't a handful of girls that would show up at the clubhouse of an outlaw motorcycle club – even if they were invited. Considering the events of our first meeting, Peyton, the newspaper reporter, probably *shouldn't* show up.

Her mouth and her attitude, however, told me she was an adventurous little bitch.

And I planned on finding out just how daring she could be.

THREE

PEYTON

I had run through many of the possibilities of what might happen when I arrived at the clubhouse – at least all of them that I could think of. Visions of Nick Navarro shoving his hand down my shorts while his MC brethren watched seemed to come to mind as being the most probable of options.

Camden was right, I was adventurous. Allowing Navarro to finger me in the bar wasn't something I would describe as typical of my behavior, though. After it was all over and I was driving home, I decided I was simply lost in the moment. Navarro's eyes were hypnotic, and with them focused on me while he was carefully tickling my g-spot, saying *no* wasn't even an option.

Truth be known, the guy could probably commit murder, and as long as he batted his insanely sexy blue eyes at the jury, they'd acquit him.

I drove around the corner, recognized the clubhouse from my Google Earth search, and slowly rolled up to the opened gate. An old warehouse that could easily pass for being abandoned was beyond the fence. In front of it, one lone motorcycle sat.

With a bare metal gas tank that was covered in rust, no front fender, and a blue and white whip dangling from one of the handlebars, it appeared to be no different than the clubhouse – abandoned.

The garage doors to the building were wide open, revealing a shop filled with miscellaneous motorcycle parts, some unidentifiable equipment, a blue steel drum, and an old refrigerator.

The early evening sunshine provided me with a false sense of security. Had it been dark, I probably would have turned around and left. But it wasn't. And I didn't.

Eager for another glimpse of Navarro's eyes – and an explanation of who he was – I pulled past the gate, parked beside the abandoned motorcycle, and got out of my Jeep. I tried to absorb as much of my surroundings as possible.

"Jeep huh? Figured you for a--"

I turned toward the gravelly voice. "Hyundai?"

He stood just beyond the open garage door, his thumbs resting inside the front pockets of his well-worn jeans. The wife beater and leather vest that he wore provided little cover, leaving his multi-colored tattoos – and his bulging biceps – in full view of my anxious eyes.

He nodded. "Something like that."

I wanted to understand more about Navarro, the brotherhood, and what attracted each of them to be in an outlaw motorcycle club. He was standing no more than ten feet from me, but it seemed that he was miles away. Having already experienced it, I preferred the face-to-face scenario we shared at the bar. I wanted to feel his breath on my lips and smell his adrenaline-infused sweat.

I pushed my hands into the pockets of my shorts and twisted my hips nervously. "So where do you want to do it?"

"Where?" He glanced around the parking lot and chuckled. "Personally, I prefer doing *it* out in the open. I'm kind of an outdoorsy fucker."

I rolled my eyes and grinned, although I fully realized my question set me up for his response. The thought of him bending me over the abandoned motorcycle made me tingle all over, but as much as I hated to, I fully realized I needed to try and keep our little meeting professional. At least for now.

"I meant the interview," I said.

"No you didn't." He raised his right hand to his chin and rubbed the growth of his beard between his thumb and forefinger as he eyed me. "You knew what you were saying had a double meaning. You did it on purpose."

I forced a laugh. It didn't sound very genuine. "For what benefit?"

He stepped closer. "You want my opinion?"

I nodded.

"Well, reporter, I think you want me to finger that little puss of yours again."

I stared back at him. My legs went weak at the thought of it. "Oh really?" I asked with a note of sarcasm in my voice.

He nodded sharply in response.

He was right, but I wasn't going to admit it. I fought against my tightening throat and eventually swallowed enough saliva to allow me to respond. "Why do you say that?"

"The last time you saw me you were wearing shorts. I stuck my finger in your tight little twat and you liked it." He took a few steps toward me, then tilted his head to the side slightly. "If you didn't like it, you'd have worn jeans today. But you didn't. You wore shorts. *Again.*"

He was now about three feet from me. I felt like the temperature had risen twenty degrees. I attempted to pry my eyes away from his, but found doing so impossible. "So, because I uhhm. Because I wore shorts,

I want you to uhhm. I want you to touch me?"

He nodded again. This time, his mouth was twisted into a smirk.

"It's summer, and we're in San Diego," I said. "Everyone wears shorts."

He took a step back and folded his arms in front of his chest. "Tell you what, little girl. If you promise to tell me the truth, and I mean always, I'll agree to an interview. How's that?"

I couldn't believe it. It was exactly what I hoped for, but in no way what I expected at least not so soon. "Sounds great," I blurted.

He extended his hand. "So, we got a deal?"

I wondered just what type of handshake he had planned. The pull me close bro hug, the soul brother web of the thumb bump with a hand-twist, or maybe slapping the palms together and then pounding knuckles? I reached for his hand slowly, not sure of what to do.

He gripped my hand in his and shook it in a conventional, gentlemanly manner.

He released my hand and shot me a serious look. "So, were you working the other day? At the bar?"

It seemed like an odd question. I answered nonetheless. "Yeah."

"And now?"

"Yeah, I suppose. Why?"

He shoved his hands into the front pockets of his jeans and cocked an eyebrow. "Not counting today and yesterday, when was the last time you wore shorts to work? Before you answer, remember, you made a deal with the devil."

I recalled no such deal. "A deal with the devil?"

"Yeah. Remember? We shook on it. And, sooner or later you'll figure it out, but I'm the devil himself," he said, his voice filled with pride.

"The devil, huh? Interesting. As far as the shorts go." I shrugged. "I don't know."

"Take a fuckin' guess."

"Never?"

He coughed out a laugh. "That's what I thought."

"You got me," I said, twisting my hips teasingly. "I wore the shorts because I liked what you did to me the other day."

He nodded as if he'd made the only point he intended to. "So, you going to take notes?"

I found his prompt changing of the topic from sexual to business abrupt and odd. I was left to wonder if he liked what we shared in the bar as much as I did. After convincing myself he was doing nothing more than playing a game with me, I responded. "I'd like to record our conversations. Are you okay with that?"

He pulled his hands from his pockets. "I prefer it," he said. "Leaves less for you to fuck up."

I noticed the fingernail on his left index finger was black. I made a mental note to ask about it later. "I don't fuck up."

"We'll see about that." He turned toward the open garage. "Follow me."

I rushed to the Jeep, grabbed my purse, and fought to catch up with him. Although I expected him to take me to an office or secret meeting room in a remote corner of the clubhouse, he sauntered up to a workbench at the far wall. With minimal effort, he hopped up onto it and sat down.

He motioned to a steel drum that was sitting beside him, kicking the top of it with the heel of his boot. "Make yourself comfortable."

The drum looked new and was remarkably clean. While wondering

HARD

if it was commonplace for bikers to use steel drums for stools, I sat down and looked around the garage. "We're uhhm. We're going to do it here?"

"What'd you expect? Starbucks and some of those crunchy little chocolate biscuits? Yeah, we're doin' it here."

I reached into my purse, pulled out my digital recorder, and held it between us.

He nodded once.

The interview began.

And Nicholas *Crip* Navarro came to life.

FOUR

NICK

She sat on the drum with her legs crossed and her forearm draped over her bare thigh. She was a gorgeous little bitch, and keeping my hands off of her went against the grain of my very existence.

I motioned toward the recorder. "Doesn't matter what we discuss, before you print anything, I proof read it. No exceptions," I said sternly. "Is that fucker on?"

"Yes, it's on. And, if those are your conditions, I'm fine with that." She raised the recorder to her mouth. "For the record, I'm Peyton Price beginning my interview with Nick Navarro, the president of the Filthy Fuckers MC. Today's date is May 7th."

I nodded. Agreeing to the interview wasn't something I did for notoriety or publicity. Making outlaw motorcycle clubs less of a target for the Department of Justice's overeager agents that seemed to infiltrate them on a daily basis was enough of a reason for me. And, if the article was written properly, the Filthy Fuckers MC could look like a bunch of choirboys.

I fixed my eyes on hers. "Get to it."

"Okay," she said. "It's obvious you're alone. I couldn't help but notice the only motorcycle here was parked beside my Jeep. It looks, well, pretty rough. Is it yours?"

"Sure is," I said with a nod. "I'm not much on electric starters, loud stereos, or windshields. Call me old school, but I'd rather kick start my sled and have the wind in my face. And a coat of paint doesn't make it any faster, so I don't have one."

She looked confused. "Sled?"

"Bike, sled, motorcycle, scoot. They all mean the same thing."

"Well, for what it's worth, I like it." She grinned. "It's unique."

"That makes two of us."

"How many men are in your club?"

"Enough to resolve any problems that we encounter."

"How long has the club been in…how long has the club been together?"

"Since the fall of 2007."

"Were you the one who founded it?"

"The one and only."

"Had you ever ridden in an MC prior to starting this one?"

I shook my head. "Nope."

"What prompted you to start the club?"

"Prompted me?"

"Yes," she said. "What in your life changed? What happened to make you feel that starting the club was in your best interest?"

"The war ended. At least for me."

"Were you a veteran?"

I cleared my throat and glared back at her. "I *am* a veteran."

"Sorry." She dropped her eyes to the floor. After a short pause, she looked up. "So, you came back from the war, and following your return, you started the club?"

"Yeah, something like that."

She scooted to the edge of the drum. Her bare legs dangled over the edge like bait. "For the sake of this and any future conversations," she said. "When I speak of an MC, I'm referring to an outlaw motorcycle club."

I shifted my eyes away from her legs and chuckled. "I'll make note of that."

"Most outlaw biker clubs are known for adhering to a set of ideals that celebrate freedom. Nonconformity to any facet of mainstream culture is also common within the ranks of MC's. After the war, did you feel the country had let you down or wronged you?"

"Nope. I was just sick and fucking tired of the bullshit – the rules, regulations, superiors. I was ready to live life without restrictions."

"And what better way to do so than start an MC?"

I clenched my fist, held it in front of her face, and slowly extended my index finger. "I don't have to answer to anyone. Society can suck my dick."

She glanced at my finger, rolled her eyes dramatically, then continued. "Regardless of your reluctance to adhere to the rules and regulations society has established, they exist nonetheless. Are you of the opinion that you're above the law?"

"Not above it, no." I shrugged. "I have my own set of rules and regulations I adhere to. I think they're enough."

"Give me an example."

"Of what?"

She placed the recorder beside me on the bench and ran her fingers through her long brown hair. "Your rules. What are they?"

I looked at the recorder, then met her gaze. I didn't have a rehearsed or published set of rules or regulations; I simply did what I felt was best under my own system of beliefs. With a *by the seat of your pants* response, I conveyed my opinion. "If you want to be left alone, keep your nose and your mitts out of my business. Don't fuck with kids, the elderly, or animals or I'll hunt your ass down. I don't know, that's about it."

She laughed. "That's it?"

I glared back at her. "What'd you expect?"

She shook her head. "I'm going to recite a handful of rules many choose to live by. I want your opinion regarding each of them."

I chuckled. "You may not like it, but I'll give it."

She pulled her phone from her pocket, tapped her fingers against the screen for a few seconds, and then began. "You shall have no other gods before Me."

"You planning on listing all ten of 'em?"

She looked surprised. "Oh. So, you're familiar with this? You recognize it?"

"I'm not some fuckin' idiot."

"I wasn't insinuating that you were. Are you a religious man?"

I shook my head. "No."

"So. Your thoughts on that? The first commandment?"

"I believe in God."

"I'm not going to list all ten," she said. "Just the ones I'm curious about."

I shrugged.

"Honor your father and your mother."

"I have a great relationship with them both."

She cleared her throat. "Thou shall not murder."

"I'll agree with that, but justifiable homicide is different."

"What act or acts justify homicide? As far as you're concerned?"

"I'll protect myself and those I care for at any cost," I said. "And back to what I said earlier. Don't fuck with kids, the elderly, or animals or I'll probably show up at your door."

"That's admirable," she said.

"What? That I don't like people who take advantage of those incapable of protecting themselves?"

She smiled and nodded. "Yes."

"When I was in school." I clenched both of my fists and raised them to my chin. "I beat the absolute shit out of kids who took advantage of other kids. You know, the kids who called others names and shit? I ran 'em down and pounded their fuckin' asses."

"You bullied bullies?"

"God damned right."

She laughed. "I like that."

"Joined the military for the same reason. I was capable of standing up for what others might not have been able to, so I did. I stood up and tried to make a difference."

"Did you?"

"Did I what?"

"Did you make a difference?" she asked.

I shook my head. "Sore subject. Next Question."

Her lips were full, her skin was without a single blemish, and her hair hung from her head like strands of brown fucking silk. Her eyes were brown, but not like any others I'd seen. They were translucent gold with little brown flecks, making them unique – at least to me. Watching them as she formulated each question was driving me insane.

"What are the differences between a riding club and an outlaw MC?"

I stared back at her. "You're gonna write a story about my club, and you don't know the fuckin' difference?"

"I do know. I want you to tell me."

"Fuck that," I growled. "You tell me your interpretation first."

After raking her fingers through her hair, she rubbed her palms together and grinned. "A riding club follows the guidelines of the American Motorcycle Association, and many are sanctioned by the AMA. Outlaw clubs don't and aren't."

I laughed. "Read that on the internet? AMA's website?"

She shook her head. "No."

She crossed one of her perfectly tanned legs over the other and then met my gaze. Slowly, I felt my cock began to stiffen.

"So, in your own words. What are the differences?" she asked.

I was done answering stupid questions about bullshit she wasn't going to use in her publication. So far, her questions were nothing more than a half-assed attempt on her part to get to know more about me. If she wanted to know who I was, showing her would be a hell of a lot easier.

It'd save us both a lot of agony in the long run.

"I'm done with this question and answer bullshit." I slid off the edge of the workbench and turned to face her.

"I'm nowhere near finished," she complained. "We're just getting started. I'll need several hours of interviews for a story."

"I wanna fuck," I said flatly.

Her eyes widened. "Excuse me?" Her expression was equal parts excitement and shock.

"All these questions are getting' under my skin. Let's fuck."

She hopped off of her makeshift seat, made eye contact with me, and cocked her hip to the side. "I'm not going to--"

"Don't even start with the innocent girl act." I reached for my belt. "Take off your shorts."

"What makes you think--"

"Ever since this little interview of yours started, you've been lookin' at me like you want to eat me. Well, here's your fuckin' chance."

"I'm not some whore. Your little finger-bang thing in the bar was--"

"Did I say you were a whore?"

"No, but--"

"I'm done talking about it. Either take off your shorts, or I will," I demanded. "All these questions are pissing me off, and your eyes are drivin' me fuckin' insane."

She chuckled a light laugh. "My eyes?"

I nodded. "Yeah, your eyes. Now get fuckin' naked."

"Let's get one thing straight," she said with a tone of authority. "If these shorts come off, it's going to be because I want them to, not because you do."

Her willingness to stand up to me wasn't something I was accustomed to, and I glared at her in disbelief. She returned my stare without an ounce of emotion. After standing in wait with a stiff cock for what seemed like forever, I broke the silence.

"Well…"

"My pussy, my rules," she said.

I chuckled. "I'm listening."

And, for the first time in as long as I could remember, I was willing to listen to what a woman had to say.

FIVE

PEYTON

I couldn't believe what I was considering. Saying *no* to Nick Navarro, however, was something I was afraid I would never be able to do. His handsome looks, tattoos, and raw essence weakened me. His remarkable blue eyes may have been partially to blame, but certainly not wholly.

The adventurous and conservative portions of my being were at war, and the adventurous side was winning.

I quickly considered my risks:

Fucking someone I was interviewing for work. I didn't believe Navarro would tell my boss – or anyone for that matter. He didn't seem like the type to brag.

Keeping my private life private after we had sex. He certainly wasn't going to fall in love with me or stalk me, so my private life would be able to remain just that – private.

STD's. There was the risk of sexually transmitted disease, but it could easily be dealt with by producing the two-year-old condom that was floating around in my purse.

I weighed the risks against the one clear benefit.

Sex with a tattooed biker. Being fucked by a bearded outlaw biker who was handsome, muscular, mature, covered in tattoos, and had a nice thick cock.

Ding, ding, ding.

We have a winner.

I reached for my purse. After digging through my wallet, I found the ancient condom. I handed it to him. "Here."

He stared at the packet as if I had handed him a foreign object. "What the fuck is this?"

"A condom."

He attempted to give it back to me. "I don't wear condoms."

I waved him off. "I won't have sex without it."

"It looks like it's too fuckin' small," he complained. "I doubt I can even get it on. Let's just fuck."

"Remember. My pussy, my rules."

His eyes narrowed to slits. "I don't even know how to operate one of these motherfuckers."

"If you want *this* pussy, you'll have to figure it out."

He bit the edge of the package and tore it open. "I'm about out of the mood."

"Shall we get back to the interview?"

"Just gimme a fuckin' minute," he growled.

I'd never spent a single moment second-guessing a choice I had made. Ever. I had always been proud of my ability to make split-second decisions and make them well. Even the serious ones were generally made quickly, and without any future remorse.

As I stood and watched Navarro fumble-fucking around with the condom, however, I couldn't help but wonder if my decision to allow him to fuck me was a good one or not. It was a spur of the moment choice made as a result of extreme desire and overwhelming curiosity. Watching him look at the condom as if he were holding a ticking time bomb wasn't very reassuring.

Or sexy.

Earlier, he said he was about out of the mood. I now shared his lack of desire.

He held the condom carefully in his left hand while he unbuckled his belt. After what appeared to be a very frustrated effort to push his jeans down to mid-thigh, he gripped his cock in his tattooed hand and began to stoke himself.

Watching him with his big dick clenched in his fist was a huge turn-on. After six or eight strokes, the massive shaft was rigid in his hand.

And, once again, I was ready.

More than ready.

"Here," I breathed. "Let me do that."

With one hand I reached for the condom, and with the other I fumbled to unbutton my shorts. After a few frustrating seconds of my own, I had my shorts on the work bench, and his cock protected by a thin layer of rubber.

"What a clusterfuck," he grumbled.

Agreed.

"Where do you, uhhm," I stammered, looking around for a place to let him fuck me.

The bench was littered in tools and motorcycle parts and the floor was covered in dirt and grease, leaving the steel drum as my only visible alternative for sex. I didn't wait for him to respond. I wrapped my arms around the drum and pressed my chest onto the lid.

"Stand up," he growled.

Oooh. Standing up sex.

Fuck yeah.

I stood up and turned to face him.

"Ditch the shirt and the bra," he demanded.

I glanced at his jeans, which were draped around his thighs. My eyes dropped to his feet. Scuffed and covered in stains, the lace-up black boots he was wearing were kind of sexy when he was fully dressed, but now that we were getting ready to fuck, they were a distraction.

I wagged my finger toward his knees. "Ditch the boots and jeans."

The glare he returned let me know he wasn't interested in considering what I wanted. He pressed his hand into the middle of my back and pushed me toward the work bench. As my hips came in contact with the cold steel, he shoved a little harder, forcing me to bend over. His hand slid from between my shoulder blades to the back of my head.

You like it rough, huh?

Yeah, me too.

He pressed my face down firmly on the top of the workbench. I felt the tip of his dick against my pussy, and inhaled sharply in anticipation. Nothing, however, could have prepared me for his girth. I wasn't ready.

At all.

He shoved me *completely* full of cock in one hard thrust.

I arched my back and gasped out in response.

His beard scraped along my neck. The warm against my cheek that followed caused goosebumps to rise along my legs. I fought to raise my head, but he was much too strong.

"I'm going to fuck you senseless," he breathed into my ear.

All concerns regarding whether or not fucking Nick Navarro was a good decision immediately vanished.

It was a *great* decision.

He thrust his hips back and forth aggressively, grunting in my ear with each stroke. "I can't…figure out…if it's my…big cock…or your… tight little pussy. But fuckin' you…is like fuckin'…a virgin."

I thought I'd been fucked by big-dicked men in the past. I was wrong. They may have been well-endowed by my standard at the time, but Nick Navarro was redefining everything.

Everything.

"I think…it's…both," I muttered.

I bit into my lip and tried to keep from crying out. I'd heard the phrase *hurts so good* many times, and only now had a complete understanding of what it meant. His thick cock was stretching my pussy to an all-new limit.

And I loved every fucking inch of it.

"I like…fucking you," he groaned. "Your little pussy clenches my cock like a vise."

Just shut up and keep fucking me.

I closed my eyes and wondered just what had happened to me. Although I was daring and bold, my interest in men was nil. Having been wronged in the past so many times, I learned to trust no one who grew facial hair.

Or had a cock.

Navarro had both and I wouldn't want him any other way.

As he pounded himself in and out of me like a man possessed, his scent filled my nostrils. It wasn't a hint of cologne or deodorant, nor was it a foul body odor.

He smelled like a man.

A *real* man.

He grabbed a fistful of my hair and pulled it taught. My back arched and my mind reeled at the thought of him fucking me like he owned me.

"Tell me how much you like this big biker cock," he growled in my ear.

Dear God.

I wanted desperately to speak, but succeeding wasn't as easy as one might think. I was suspended somewhere between heaven and earth, and talking wasn't an option.

He pulled against my hair until his lips met my ear. His warm breath on my neck made my legs go weak. "Say something, you sexy little bitch."

If you keep talking dirty to me, I'm going to explode.

I opened my mouth, but...*nothing.*

"Newspaper reporter my ass," he breathed. "You came here for my cock, didn't you?"

I did my best to nod, but his tight grip on my hair made doing so close to impossible.

"I uhhm." I stammered.

He bit into my earlobe. "Didn't you?" he grunted.

"Yes," I breathed.

I told myself it wasn't true, but at that moment, I wasn't completely sure. Between his savage thrusts, I decided it was the thrill of actually being fucked by Navarro that attracted me, and nothing more.

Nick Navarro may have been a lot of different things to a lot of different people. To me, he was an outlaw biker.

Having him fuck me was taking me to a place I had never ventured to.

A place I was afraid I would yearn to return to, over and over.

While he continued to fuck me like he was attempting to prove a point, he wedged his tattooed forearm between my hip and the bench.

In a few seconds, I felt the tip of his finger circling my throbbing clit.

"You're gonna come back for this cock whenever I want you to."

Don't worry about that, big boy.

Until further notice, this pussy's yours.

I wanted to give a smart-assed response, but couldn't seem to assemble my thoughts. As he rubbed my swollen nub and repeatedly filled me with his dick, my mind drifted off to a faraway place.

After an immeasurable amount of time, a tingling began to run through me. Immediately following, his cock seemed to double in size. I fought against the pressure of his hand against my head, but eventually gave up. His hips slammed against my ass a few more times, and my pussy went into a thankful frenzy of its own.

His thrusts slowed, but remained os-so-deep. His breathing became irregular.

And.

An orgasm shot through my body like a bolt of lightning.

And then another.

And another.

"Fuck yesss," he moaned.

"Oh…My…God," I cried out.

While my body continued to convulse in the wake of countless earth-shattering micro-orgasms, I collapsed.

My vision narrowed as he withdrew himself from inside of me. The sounds of the distant traffic, his breathing, and my heart beating became dull and indifferent.

In short, Nick Navarro – and his big cock – changed my mind about everything.

SIX

NICK

I stared at the exterior wall of the shop, not sure whether to get off my bike, or fire it up and go for a ride. Peyton Price had my interest – and my attention – and I didn't like it one fucking bit.

She was a sexy little bitch, but I had no business with a woman in my clubhouse or on my mind, no matter how attractive she was. While contemplating a ride up the PCH, the unmistakable lyrics from Cypress Hill's *How I Could Just Kill a Man* blaring over the rumble of Pee Bee's loud pipes snapped me out of my funk.

I turned toward the sound.

With his long legs stretched out onto his floorboards, and his arms draped over his handlebars, he leisurely rolled into the lot.

"What's shakin', Motherfucker?" he said as he came to a stop at my side.

I shrugged.

"Comin' or goin'?"

"Thinkin' about havin' a beer," I responded.

"Sounds good."

I nodded toward the shop. "Of all the shit you could be listening to, you've got to listen to *that* song?"

He pulled off his helmet and ran his fingers through his long hair.

"Cypress motherfuckin' Hill, Boss. It's good shit.".

"*How I Could Just Kill a Man.* Remind you of anything?"

"Sure as fuck does," he responded.

I gave him my signature look. A cocked eyebrow. I'd used it so much over the years that one side of my forehead was wrinkled, and the other wasn't.

"That night Wood dumped his bike in front of that mansion up by Torrey Pines."

Pee Bee may have been absent minded when it came to the passage of time, and his sheer size alone removed fear from the list of emotions he felt, but other than that, he was real damned close to normal.

Most of the time.

"What in the fuck does Wood hitting a fox in Torrey Pines have to do with that song?"

He looked at me as if I was a complete fool. "Wood hit the fox. Then that chick in the nightgown came out to see if we were okay. While she was tryin' to get Wood bandaged up, I was starin' at her tits and flippin' through my iPod for something cool to listen to. I saw Cypress Hill, and thought it sounded good. So, that's what I was listenin' to the whole time she was standin' there with her titties pokin' out of that nightgown."

The owner of the thirty-million-dollar mansion was the widow of a Hollywood producer, and built like a porn star. In a sheer nightgown and a pair of designer flip-flops, she rushed from the house and offered to bandage Wood's arm. The entire time, her silicone D-cups were all but hanging out of her nightgown. It was a story we'd talked about for years, but it had nothing to do with what was now on my mind.

I got off my bike and turned toward the shop. "Well it reminds me of something else."

"Like what?"

I unlocked the door, opened it, and motioned toward the steel drum. "We need to get rid of that body."

"Still in that drum?"

I shot him a glare. "Where the fuck else would it be?"

"Fuck, I don't know. That's why I asked."

"Do you really think I'd take that two-hundred-pound dead prick out of that drum and do something with him?" I asked. "He's been in there cooking for three days."

"Two."

"It's been three."

"Been two." He looked at his watch. "Today's Monday the 9th. Wedding was on Saturday the 7th."

Peyton had started her recording by saying, *I'm Peyton Price beginning my interview with Nick Navarro, the president of the Filthy Fuckers MC. Today's date is May 7th.*

"You sure it's the 9th?"

He glanced at his watch and nodded.

If her assembly of facts was as inaccurate as her telling of time, I wouldn't approve a single word to go to publication.

"What?" he asked. "You got to be somewhere?"

I shook my head. As we walked toward the refrigerator, I considered telling him about Peyton, reconsidered it, and then decided to tell him a shortened version of the truth. "That reporter chick came in here yesterday and interviewed me. The one from the bar. When she started her interview, she said it was the 7th. It wasn't. It was the 8th. No big deal."

He grabbed two bottles of beer and handed me one. "Bitch might not know what day it is, but she's hot as fuck."

I nodded. "She's a sexy little bitch."

He tossed his lid into the trash. "You fuck her?"

I opened my beer and took a long drink.

"You fucked her, didn't you?" He shook his head. "I swear, young bitches flock to your old ass."

I raised the bottle to my mouth and shrugged. "Young chicks dig old men."

"Since when?" he snapped back.

"Since forever. With age comes maturity." I tilted the neck of my beer bottle toward him. "Maturity brings comfort."

He choked on his beer. After wiping his mouth on the back of his hand, he returned a dramatic glare. "Comfort in what?"

"They know an old man will give 'em a good honest fucking. No lies, no unmet promises, no pick-up lines. Just a lot of hard cock."

"And that's enough to keep 'em happy?"

I waved my arms toward the empty shop. "You see any women in here complaining?"

"Nope."

"That's because I never told 'em I loved 'em, but I always fucked 'em like I did."

"She suck good cock?" he asked. "Bitch has got some serious DSL's."

"Dunno."

"She didn't suck your cock?"

"She was askin' me question after question, and I'm sittin' on the bench listenin' to her, and trying my fuckin' damndest to stay focused," I explained. "But she's wearin' shorts, some Chuck's, and a tight tee shirt. And she kept running her fingers through her fuckin' hair. Bitch was driving me nuts. Next thing I know, I'm sittin' right there with a fuckin' chubby."

I motioned toward the bench with my beer bottle.

"Where was she?"

"Sittin' on the drum."

He glared back at me in disbelief. "You had her sittin' on Whip's dead brother?"

I grinned and nodded. "Didn't want her sittin' beside me. You know how I am about havin' people in my space."

"Where'd you fuck her?"

"Bent her over the bench."

He coughed out a laugh. "Just couldn't fuck her while she was hovering over a corpse?"

"I didn't give a fuck if she sat on him, but I didn't want to fuck her while she was layin' her tits on him."

"Makes sense."

The things that made sense to a biker were undoubtedly different than what made sense to most people in the free world. I could tell any of the men in the club that I had a body to dispose of, and their response would be *where is it?* If the same question was asked of someone out of my group, most people would respond by vomiting.

Or calling the cops.

Our MC consisted of a close-knit group of men who would place their lives on the line for any of their club brothers. The comradery and devotion was as close to what I felt in the Navy. Often, my MC brethren reminded me of my SEAL team.

"So, that's something we need to get taken care of quick. Today, if possible."

"What's that?"

"The body in that fuckin' drum."

"Wanna do it now?"

"No. We're gonna need to drive out to the desert. Or up to Temecula, by the mountains. Fucker's been in that drum of Sodium Hydroxide since Saturday night, I'd say he's about ready."

"Acid's the way to go, huh?"

"Sodium Hydroxide's not acid. It's lye. They use acid on T.V., but in real life, the shit doesn't work. The fumes alone from hydrochloric or hydrofluoric would kill you. And it doesn't do what they show it doing on T.V., believe me."

His face distorted. "How the fuck you know all this shit?"

I tapped my index finger against the tattoo on my bicep of the eagle, anchor, trident, and pistol – the insignia of the SEALs.

"Shoulda known," he said.

"They didn't just teach us how to kill, they taught us how to do it and not leave a trace," I said with a laugh.

He tossed his empty beer bottle in the trash. "Funny. Government teaches you how to do that shit, and the same government will lock you up for doing what they trained you for."

"Don't get me started." I waved my hand toward the fridge. "Grab me one, too."

He opened the two beers, handed me one of them, and kicked the steel drum with the toe of his boot. "So we just pour him out on the ground?"

"It's gonna be a fuckin' mess," I explained. "We need to dump it somewhere, scavenge what's left of the bones, and crush 'em up. They'll be pretty brittle. And hollow."

"Figure out when, and I'm good to go," he said.

"You ought to be, you dip-shit. Who doesn't leave air holes when they do something like that?"

"Well, Mr. Navy fucking SEAL, not all of us are special warfare experts. That's the first motherfucker to ever have his face taped up by me. So, considering, I think I did a pretty good job," he said in a prideful tone.

"You did a damned fine job, Peeb. Just fell a little short on keepin' the fucker alive," I said with a laugh.

"Fuck this prick. He swung a baseball bat at my head." He kicked his boot against the drum. "If it wasn't for my cat-like reflexes, you'd be buryin' me in the desert, not him."

I raised my beer bottle. "I'm just fuckin' with ya."

"Seriously, though. What are we gonna do about these pricks?"

"The Savages?"

He nodded. "Yeah."

"We both know they're tryin' to force us out, because they've been here longer. I haven't got much interest in dissolving the club. You?"

"Nope."

"So, we stand our ground. Sooner or later, they'll back off. If they don't, we go to war."

"I'm tired of lookin' over my shoulder every fuckin' time I hear a set of pipes comin' down the road."

"You and me both, Brother. You and me both," I said.

"So what about this newspaper chick? You done with the interview?"

I shook my head. "Just getting started."

"So she's gonna be comin' around for a bit?"

"A long bit."

The words escaped my mouth before I had much time to think about my response. It was apparent from what Peyton said about the amount of hours she would need to invest in interviews that she would be around for some time. In my opinion, exposing her to a limited amount of the club's activities would help matters as much, if not more, than interviews.

Like it or not, if I wanted a favorable portrayal of the club in the newspaper, it was something that going to require a significant amount of time on her part, and mine.

My fear was knowing I wouldn't be able to keep my cock out of her. In reality, I was a Filthy Fucker in more ways than one.

I raised my bottle of beer. "Filthy Fuckers forever."

Pee Bee raised his and clanked it against mine. "Forever Filthy Fuckers."

Truer words had never been spoken.

SEVEN

PEYTON

After downloading the files from my recorder to my laptop, I started listening to the interview. Typing a rough outline of my story was something I always tried to do when information and events were fresh in my mind, and Nick Navarro was still fresh in my mind.

Very much so. It was twenty-four hours after the interview, and I still felt like he was inside of me.

I crossed my legs as I heard his raspy voice come through the earbuds.

After a moment or two of reminiscing, I fast-forwarded through the beginning of the interview. After skimming through a few of the questions, one portion of the questions and answers caught my attention.

"Most outlaw biker clubs are known for adhering to a set of ideals that celebrate freedom. Nonconformity to any facet of mainstream culture is also common within the ranks of MC's. After the war, did you feel the country had let you down or wronged you?"

"Nope. I was just sick and fucking tired of the bullshit – the rules, regulations, superiors. I was ready to live life without restrictions."

"And what better way to do so than start an MC?"

"I don't have to answer to anyone. Society can suck my dick."

I pressed the *pause* tab, typed a few notes about Navarro, and continued to listen. Minutes later, and I was more than halfway through the interview.

"*When I was in school, I beat the absolute shit out of kids who took advantage of other kids. You know, the kids who called others names and shit? I ran 'em down and pounded their fuckin' asses.*"

"You bullied bullies?"

"*God damned right.*"

"I like that."

I pressed *pause* again, made a few notes, and typed a paragraph about Navarro's soft side. As the recording's topic of conversation changed from outlaw MC's to sex, it dawned on me that I didn't turn the recorder off.

Surely it didn't...

"*I'm going to fuck you senseless,*" I heard him growl.

Then, his gravelly voice continued. "*I can't...figure out...if it's my... big cock...or your...tight little pussy. But fuckin' you...is like fuckin'...a virgin.*"

I listened to the sound of him fucking me until it felt like my pussy was on fire, and then I turned off the recording and pulled the earbuds from my ears. My eyes darted around my bedroom as if the answer to why my pussy was dripping down my leg was somewhere amidst my collection of snowboards, surfboards, and skateboards.

The thought of having Navarro's strong hand on the back of my head while his scent filled my nostrils seemed to consume me. I realized a full-fledged biker wasn't the desire of all women, but his tattoos, muscles, raspy voice, and manner of dress were sexy as hell.

Who was I kidding? Everything about him was sexy.

As ridiculous as it seemed, I felt the need to see him again.

Immediately. Knowing what he was sexually capable of and not taking advantage of it was a waste; whether he understood it as such or not.

I didn't have his phone number, and the only way I knew to find him was to either go to the bar or drop by the clubhouse. Even if he wasn't at the clubhouse, I knew I may encounter other members of the club, and the probability of obtaining some useful information was high.

I had little doubt that an uninvited stop at the clubhouse would get me into trouble with Navarro.

Probably *big* trouble.

The clubhouse it is.

Rolling down the freeway, ten minutes away from my exit, I began to fill with remorse for making the decision to go see him. While stuck in traffic, I reached toward the passenger seat, fumbled inside my purse for a moment, and removed the recorder.

I turned down the radio, pressed *play*, then fast-forwarded to the action.

"Say something, you sexy little bitch." The almost inaudible sound of his whisper caused me to almost hit the car in front of me. I stomped my foot against the brakes, causing the Jeep to come to an abrupt stop.

"Newspaper reporter my ass, you came here for my cock, didn't you?"

"I uhhm."

"Didn't you?"

"Yes."

The sound of his voice was such a turn-on.

I had no business going to his clubhouse unannounced, but to be an effective reporter, I needed a realistic means of getting in touch with him, and I had no means short of hunting him down.

Convinced the drive to the warehouse was my only option, I considered viable options that I could explain which would support my need to see him with such urgency.

I have a few questions regarding the club's process of initiating prospects.

How many miles, on average, do you ride a year?

Do your members also have other means of transportation?

Does the club have a means of income, or is it self-supporting through dues and contributions?

Does the club participate in charitable events?

Shit.

None of the questions were critical for my first installment on the piece, and Navarro would see right through me.

I felt like such a girl.

I'd be much better off just telling him the truth.

I exited the highway, came to a stop at the traffic light, and then slowly proceeded down the street toward the clubhouse. When I got close enough to get an unobstructed view of the building, I could clearly see that there were three motorcycles parked in front.

I envisioned a secret meeting, drug deal, or weapons transaction going down. I considered driving past, but curiosity got the best of me. I turned through the gate, drove slowly toward the front of the building, and came to a stop beside Navarro's eclectic example of a motorcycle.

I grabbed my recorder and pushed the door to the Jeep open.

"I don't recall giving you a standing invite to stop by my clubhouse at will, reporter."

I turned toward the voice, but saw no one. I responded nonetheless. "You didn't."

Be assertive, Peyton.

Take charge.

I scanned the empty garage. Navarro was nowhere to be found. I cleared my throat. "But if you want this article to make your club look good in the eyes of all who read it, I suggest you cooperate with the woman who is writing the article."

Navarro stepped from inside the garage and stood ten feet in front of me with his arms folded in front of his chest. Dressed in a pair of well-worn jeans, boots, and a black wife-beater, he looked every bit the part of a biker. He raised his right hand to his face, clenched his fist, and exhaled into the void between his thumb and forefinger.

With his eyes locked on me, he inhaled a long slow breath, then lowered his fist. Without so much as saying a word, his extremely commanding presence seemed to suck the confidence from my very soul.

I was left standing in front of him feeling small, helpless, and without a single thought of my own.

I was his for the taking.

I turned my head to the side and swallowed heavily, hoping he didn't notice. As I turned to face him, I feigned a cough, then met his gaze. "I need your phone number."

He continued to stare. "You *want* my phone number. You don't *need* it."

I straightened my posture and cleared my throat. "Upon returning home from the war, Nicholas *Crip* Navarro formed a band of hand-selected brothers not much different than the men who fought at his side during the eight-year-long protracted armed conflict in Iraq."

His face expressed not one ounce of emotion.

I maintained eye contact and continued. "To the layman, the differences between his military and state-side brethren were crystal clear. To Navarro, the five-foot-eleven, 200 pound tattooed war veteran – and president of the Filthy Fuckers Motorcycle Club – there were no differences. To understand the similarities in the men, one must be able to peer well beyond the surface of the club's members. Navarro gave me a look deep inside the makings of his club, and after doing so, I was able to see the members not for who and what they appeared to be, but for who they truly were."

"You done?" he asked.

I shook my head. "If war broke out in these United States tomorrow, and I was in charge of my own well-being, the US Marines nor the Army would have the honor of defending me. I'd make one phone call, and one only – to Navarro. And after that call, I'd drift off into a deep slumber, knowing no harm would come to me."

His mouth curled into a shitty little smirk.

"You know the only problem with that story?" I asked.

"Nope."

"I couldn't make that one phone call. Because I don't have your fucking phone number."

"You know my only problem I've got with you being at my clubhouse, reporter?"

I shrugged. "Uhhm. I guess not."

"Every time you open your pretty little mouth, all I can think about is shoving my cock in it."

I was flattered.

Kind of.

"I don't know whether to say thank you, or fuck you."

He chuckled. "I like your attitude. The number's 619 447 1035. And no, I won't repeat it."

Six, one, nine, four, four seven, one, zero, three, five. Six, one, nine, four, four seven, one, zero, three, five. Six, one, nine, four, four seven, one, zero, three, five. Six, one, nine, four, four seven, one, zero, three, five.

"I don't need to write it down, I'm a reporter."

Six, one, nine, four, four seven, one, zero, three, five.

He nodded. "Impressive. How's the article coming?"

"Just getting started," I responded. "We need to, uhhm, meet again. Soon."

Six, one, nine, four, four seven, one, zero, three, five.

I studied him. His clothes served him all too well. His shirt hugged his muscular torso like a black glove, leaving nothing about his washboard stomach and massive chest to the imagination. His worn denim jeans were tight against his shapely butt, more proof that all of his leisure time wasn't spent in the bar.

His ass was the product of countless hours at the gym.

Charlie Hunnam was no longer the object of my sexual desire.

Nick Navarro was.

"I'm busy right now, reporter," he said. "Give me a shout tomorrow, around noon. Maybe we can have coffee and a crunchy little biscuit. How's that sound?"

Six, one, nine, four, four seven, one, zero, three, five.

"Alright," I said, turning away. "Talk to you tomorrow."

I opened the door to the Jeep, climbed inside, and did an imaginary fist pump.

Yes!

HARD

And, the entire drive home, all I could think of was him shoving his cock in my mouth every time I started to speak.

EIGHT

NICK

I turned into the coffee shop, coasted to a stop, and parked the bike alongside a hybrid Toyota. In complete contrast to most of my southern California neighbors, I tried like hell to leave the biggest carbon footprint on the earth that I could.

I hopped off my bike and glanced at the battery-powered eco-friendly ride. From the rearview mirror, an orange dangled by a string. Protruding from the skin of the fruit over the entire surface, were cloves.

A hippie air freshener.

Today's colon-cleansing, environmentally conscious, trash-separating robots disgusted me. I felt if the occupants of the earth could focus more on being genuine, and less on being what they felt others expected them to be, the world would be a much better place.

I scanned the lot for Peyton's Jeep, but saw nothing. After checking my watch, I realized I was ten minutes early. I gazed out into the street, wondering if I could stomach being in the presence of whoever drove the fruit-scented Prius until she arrived. In a matter of seconds, she swerved between two passing cars and into the parking lot.

With the top off of her Jeep and Jimi Hendrix's *Castles Made of Sand* playing loud enough that I could recognize it, she shot into an empty stall, parked, and hopped out of the Jeep. Wearing her trademark attire of jean shorts, Chuck's, and a tee shirt, she looked no differently than she had on the other three occasions I had seen her.

"Nice day for going topless," I said.

She pulled her hair into a ponytail and secured it with a rubber band from her wrist. "Your subliminal suggestions are falling on deaf ears, biker man."

"It was worth a try, *reporter*."

While walking toward me, she dropped her sunglasses in her purse, removed a pair of glasses, and put them on.

One of my weaknesses was a hot bitch wearing glasses. With her hair in a ponytail and the bold black frames fixed high on the bridge of her nose, my imagination took over. An image of her peering at me through the lenses while my cock was in her mouth quickly came to mind.

"You wear glasses?"

"My contacts were killing my eyes."

I admired her until she was at my side, then turned toward the entrance. "Inside or outside?"

She stepped between me and the Toyota. "Outside."

We got our drinks, she declined a crunchy biscuit, and we sat outside at a table amongst several coffee-drinking sun worshipers.

"So, did you remember my number?" I asked.

"Six, one, nine, four, four seven, one, zero, three, five."

"Good memory, huh?"

She laughed. "Like a fucking elephant."

"What was so fuckin' important that you had to come by the shop last night?"

She looked embarrassed for a split-second, but quickly donned a smile. "I was working on the piece, and realized I had no way to get ahold of you. I can't effectively write something informative if my only way of obtaining information is by simply stumbling into you."

"How many more times are we going to have to meet?"

After I asked the question, I realized sooner or later, the meetings between us would actually end. As much as I never would have guessed it, the thought of not seeing her again wasn't something I looked forward to.

"I don't know," she responded. "Maybe ten or twelve."

"Ten or twelve?" I snapped back. "Jesus."

"Well, four installments." She took a drink of coffee, then shrugged. "Three or so meetings for each article. It's not that much."

"Guess not."

She pulled the recorder from her purse. "You want to do a little more now?"

I wondered what else she might ask, and was anxious to find out. "Might as well."

She glanced over each shoulder, raised her hand to her mouth, and spoke. "For the record, I'm Peyton Price conducting my second interview with Nick Navarro, the president of the Filthy Fuckers MC. Today's date is May 11th."

She placed the recorder on the table between us. "Are you single?"

I nodded. "Have been since, shit…for ten years."

"Is your refusal to be in a committed relationship a result of not trusting women?"

"I didn't say I refused to be in a committed relationship. I just said I wasn't in one." I said. "And it's not about trusting women, I don't trust myself."

HARD

"You don't trust yourself? Can you explain?"

I glanced at the woman seated beside us. Long, lean, and tan, she appeared to be in her mid-forties. Her fake tits were bulging from her designer top, and her hands were covered in jewels. Although she sat with who I suspected was her husband, her focus was clearly our conversation. Her eyes dropped to my boots, and slowly raised

"Here's the issue," I said. "I like pussy. A lot."

She wrinkled her nose and stared. "So much that it's a problem?"

"Prevents me being in a committed relationship, that's for sure. I might be a lot of things, but I'm not a liar." I shifted my eyes to the skinny bitch seated beside us, who was still ear hustling our conversation. "So I just fuck the shit out of every girl I meet, but make sure they're well aware that all they're gettin' is my cock."

She cleared her throat. "I think she's with someone."

I turned to face Peyton. "She'd take it if I was offering."

"Seriously?"

I nodded. "Believe me."

"Would you give it to her?"

I grinned a mischievous smile. "I sure would. And I'd make you hold her skinny ass down while I did it."

"I don't think so," she snapped back.

I looked at the skinny bitch. She shot me a curious look while her husband poked his finger against the screen of his phone.

Peyton knocked her knuckles on the edge of the table. "See if you can stay focused on the interview."

I shifted my focus back to her and chuckled. "I'll do my best."

"Have any kids?"

None that I know of.

"Nope."

"Do you have a mode of transportation for foul weather days? Anything other than the *sled*?"

"Nope."

"Your thoughts on transgender bathrooms?"

"Excuse me?"

"A person with a sexual identity that differs from their assigned sexuality. Transgender. Where should they go to the bathroom?"

"Wherever they fuckin' want to. People need to worry more about themselves and their fuckin' kids, and stop worrying about what everyone else is doing or not doing."

"Do you believe in equality?"

I believe I want to shove my cock down your throat.

"I believe it doesn't exist."

"Should it?" she asked.

"Sure as fuck should."

"On earth and in your club? Or only where it's convenient?"

"Everywhere."

"It's common knowledge that the guidelines for the Hells Angels MC prohibit black membership. The Bandidos and Mongols MC's share this guideline. In fact, a 2008 federal indictment listed many racist acts that were allegedly committed by the Mongol's members, including beatings and murder. Do the guidelines of your club allow black members?"

"Generally speaking, there are black MC's and there are white MC's. The FFMC is an MC that chooses not to discriminate."

"Do you have any black members?"

"No."

She widened her eyes. "Will you ever?"

HARD

"If a man wants to prospect with the club, and he's a solid dude, we'll consider it. If he passes the initiation without problems, he'll be a patched-in member. Skin color has nothing to do with our decision making process."

"What, specifically, is the initiation process?"

I admired her for a moment. She was beautiful by anyone's standards. With the glasses on, she was irresistible. As I felt my cock began to go stiff, I pressed the heel of my palm against it.

I exhaled heavily. "By invitation from a fully-patched member, someone becomes a *hang-around*. A hang-around is a person that comes to club functions by invitation only, and only with the member who vouched for him. After some time, say, after six months, they may become an *associate*. An associate is a glorified hang-around. Maybe they'll attend a few organized rides with us, go to a few parties, and hang around the clubhouse – again, by invitation only. Then, if agreed by the membership of the club. They may become a *prospect*. If so, they prospect with the club for a year, and then must receive a unanimous vote for membership."

"So, the process takes eighteen months?"

I nodded. "At least."

"Have you denied anyone membership?"

"Yes."

"Who and why?"

"*Who* is none of your god damned business. *Why*? Because they weren't capable."

"Capable of what?"

I considered my response, and gave one that lacked specifics, but was revealing enough to keep her from continuing. "He wasn't capable of satisfying every member of the club that he was who we needed."

She nodded, took a drink of her coffee, and gazed beyond me for a moment. After zoning out for some time, she met my gaze. "Your club, no differently than other outlaw MC's, claims territory. Often, when many clubs claim the same territory, there's *bickering* between the clubs. Does the FFMC have *issues* with any clubs? Do you have a rival?"

"Off the record, there are always issues with someone. On the record. No."

She reached for the recorder, turned it off, and cocked an eyebrow. "Off the record."

I shrugged. It was no secret that FFMC and Satan's Savages were rivals. "Off the record, Satan's Savages are poking around where they shouldn't be."

She nodded and pushed her glasses up the bridge of her nose.

I locked eyes with her. "Take off those glasses."

She grinned. "Why?"

"Because I want to fuck your pretty little mouth when I look at you. Take 'em off."

"I can't see without them."

"And I can't promise you I'll keep my cock in my pants if you leave 'em on."

"So, you're going to mouth rape me if I choose to wear them?"

I chuckled. "Pretty tough to rape a willing mouth."

"Who says my mouth is willing?"

"I just did."

She tried to look surprised at my claim. It didn't work.

She scrunched her brow. "Based on what?"

I stood from my seat, stepped to her side, and pressed my mouth against her ear. "I want you to suck my big cock, reporter."

She didn't respond.

"Did you hear me?" I growled.

She nodded, and an almost inaudible *uh huh* escaped her lips.

"I want to feel those full lips of yours wrapped around it while you dig your nails into my ass. I want you to force so much of it down your throat that your fuckin' eyes water," I whispered.

"I uhhm. I…"

"So, you don't want it? You don't want to suck my big fucking dick?"

"Uhhm. No," she murmured.

I reached below the table and slowly dragged my finger along her inner thigh, giving her plenty of time to resist. After no such protest, I forced my finger beneath the denim of her shorts and slid it into her soaking wet pussy.

"You're drenched, reporter. It appears your twat doesn't agree with that bullshit your mouth is trying to sell me. Your wet little pussy wants you to suck my cock."

"We can't keep doing this."

I pulled my finger from inside of her and wiped it on the thigh of my jeans. "Doing what? We're just talking."

"We're…uhhm…we're…" she stammered.

I sat down and took a drink of my coffee. "We're talking. I thought that's what you wanted. To talk."

Her glasses were askew on her face, one side sitting much lower than the other. Probably a result of me pressing my cheek against hers, but seeing her appear unkempt was satisfying in its own regard.

"Fix your glasses, reporter. They're crooked."

She took off her glasses, scowled at me, then placed them back on her face perfectly.

She reached for the recorder, tossed it into her purse, and sighed. "We're done for the day. Now, I want a ride on your motorcycle. For the sake of the article, of course."

"God damned shame I don't have a helmet you can wear. State law requires passengers to wear 'em."

"Oh really?" she asked.

"Yep. Hell, if I had one for you, I'd give you a ride. Might be uncomfortable, but it'd be a ride."

"So the helmet's all that's keeping you from it?"

I had no desire to give her a ride, but I nodded anyway. "Yep."

"Good." She stood up. "I've got my Biltwell in the Jeep. Let me get it."

I stood up. "Your what?"

She took off toward her Jeep in light jog.

"Helmet," she responded over her shoulder.

Fuck.

I wondered why in the fuck she'd have a helmet in her Jeep, but was afraid to ask.

"It's got to be DOT approved," I shouted.

"It is." She leaned into the back of the Jeep and quickly produced a gold and burgundy helmet. "I bought it for snowboarding, but it's a motorcycle helmet."

"You snowboard?"

She turned around, removed her glasses, and pulled the helmet down over her head. "Yep. Snowboard, skateboard, surf, rock climb, bungie jump. If it makes my heart pound, I'll do it."

Crazy little bitch.

She put her glasses back on. "Ready?"

I pointed to my bike. "I'm a man of my word."

But at that particular moment, I wished I wasn't.

NINE

PEYTON

Riding on the back of the motorcycle was exactly what Navarro said it would be. Uncomfortable. Although the motorcycle was designed to carry two people, he had modified it to carry only one, leaving a slight piece of leather on the rear fender for a passenger to sit on. Even at that, it was much better than skateboarding, far more satisfying than surfing, and was a close second only to snowboarding.

Having my arms wrapped around his waist made what would have been extremely uncomfortable seem almost sensual. The vibration from the V-twin engine did the rest. It felt like I was riding a 600-pound vibrator, and having Nick Navarro's muscular torso in my hands made matters that much better.

The sound from the pipes as he shifted the gears was a reminder of the power that was wedged between my thighs. I found the entire experience thrilling, and realized as we slowed to as stop that even if Navarro never wanted to give me a ride again, the thrill-seeking part of me would forever yearn for another taste.

He tilted his head toward a bar at the intersection. "Want to grab a bite at this bar?"

"Sure," I shouted.

"It's a biker bar.

"I'm okay with that."

He nodded and released the clutch lever. "They've got good burgers."

Although I had my purse – and my recorder – I had no intention of ruining our lunch by interviewing him. A simple discussion over lunch would be nice, even if he didn't think so.

I realized figuring out who Navarro *really* was may not ever happen, but obtaining a closer look into his life was an exciting addition to mine, that was for sure.

He pulled into the parking lot, turned the motorcycle around, and parked backward in the parking stall, facing the street. Short of his motorcycle and a few other cars, the parking lot was empty.

He switched the ignition to *off*. Even in the absence of the engine running, my legs, ass, and pussy continued to vibrate. "I *really* like riding on this thing."

He removed his helmet. "Cheapest therapy money can buy."

I took off my glasses and unbuckled my helmet. "Can I leave this out here?"

"Just hang it on the handlebars. Nobody fucks with helmets on a Harley."

"Why?"

He cocked an eyebrow. "Do I look like a nice guy?"

I shook my head. "Not really."

"That's why."

I hung my helmet on the handlebars. "Nothing we talk about here is for publication, by the way. This is all off the record."

He ran his fingers through his hair and nodded. "Good to know."

"I do have some questions, though."

He turned toward the door. "Ask away."

"Why do you park backward?"

"What do you mean?"

"Well, if you were in a car, you'd park facing the building. But you parked facing the street."

"When we're ready to leave, all we've got to do is fire that pig up and go. It only goes in one direction, forward. So if I was facing the building, I'd have to push it around to face the street before we could go. Doing it when you park makes leaving, I don't know, *easier*."

"A quick getaway?"

He pulled the door open, motioned toward the open bar, and chuckled. "Something like that."

Surprised that he opened the door, I promptly thanked him. "Thank you."

The bar resembled the bar I met him in. It was dark and void of any wait staff. Two rough looking men sat at the bar drinking beer, and they were the only patrons I could see.

"Out of curiosity, how'd you find me on that first day?" he asked.

"I'm a reporter. We investigate things."

"Just like a junior fucking federal agent, huh?"

"No," I said. "Like a private investigator."

"Same fucking thing." He stepped up to the bar. "What do you want?"

I shrugged. "Whatever's good. Order for me?"

"Pete, give me two burger specials and two bottles of Budweiser."

Oh my God. Budweiser.

Barf.

The bartender opened two bottles of beer and handed them to Navarro. "Burger's will be right up, Nick. Anything else?"

HARD

"Nope. Appreciate ya," Navarro said with a nod.

He handed me one of the bottles of beer. "Table or booth?"

I took a drink. It was better than I expected. "Booth."

I followed him to a booth in the rear of the bar and sat down. "Riding on that thing is addictive."

He picked at the label on his bottle. "Sure is."

"You know what they say about people who pick at their beer labels, don't you?"

"Guess not."

"They're sexually frustrated."

"Sounds about right."

"You're sexually frustrated?"

He grinned. "Take off your glasses, and I'll be fine."

I took a drink of beer and returned a smile. "Suffer."

I fully realized it had been less than a week, but he had already fingered me, fucked me and brought me to climax no less than half a dozen times – counting the two times I masturbated while thinking of him – and I felt like we were developing an odd friendship as a result.

"Believe me, I am," he said with a smile.

Seeing him smile was rewarding. The image he portrayed naturally was one of a rough, take-no-shit biker. His smile revealed perfectly situated white teeth, and seeing them convinced me that the true Nicholas Navarro was much more than what was seen on the surface.

"Maybe one day, if you don't piss me off--"

"What? You'll take 'em off? Or you're gonna suck my cock?"

I shrugged. "Maybe both."

He raised his bottle of beer and grinned. "I'll wait patiently."

I couldn't believe how easy it was for me to offer myself to him, but being in his presence made me do all of the things that I told myself in his absence I wouldn't continue to do. He undoubtedly brought out the best of my worst decisions.

The sound of motorcycles in the parking lot made me wonder if some of his FFMC brethren had seen his motorcycle and were stopping in for a beer. We both looked out the window at the same time, and I noticed two men wearing leather vests parking their motorcycles. The look on Navarro's face, however, told me whoever had shown up wasn't someone he wanted to see.

He stood from his seat and turned to face me. His look was stern, serious, and one of actual concern. "No matter what happens, don't get out of that seat until this is over."

"Until what's over? Who is it?"

"God damn it," he bellowed. "Stay right *here*. Do you understand me?"

I fought against my tightening throat. "I understand. Yes, Sir."

"Stay right there," he said in a demanding tone. "I fucking mean it."

I swallowed hard. "Okay."

"Pete! Got two Savages at the door!" he shouted.

Oh shit.

Upon hearing the announcement, the two men seated at the bar got off of their stools and walked toward the back of the bar. I pulled the recorder from my purse, turned it on, and placed it on the edge of the table.

Navarro took a few steps toward the door, stopped and glanced over his shoulder. As our eyes met, he winked.

Seriously?

Did you just fucking wink at me?

Two pretty rough looking men – one of which was roughly Navarro's size – walked through the front door. The other man was slightly shorter, but built like a weight-lifter. The shorter of the two men had a shaved head. The taller had tattoos on his neck and all-over-the-place brown hair.

"Looks like you might have picked the wrong place for lunch, Whip," Navarro said. "Get back on your sled and go somewhere else."

The bigger of the two had *Whip* and *President* on his vest. The other man's vest said *Panda*, and *Sergeant-At-Arms*.

Whip stopped a few steps in front of Navarro. Panda stood beside him. Both men were facing me, and Navarro's back was to me.

"Where's my brother?" Whip asked.

Navarro chuckled. "Out fuckin' a goat somewhere?"

"I'm not gonna ask you again," Whip growled.

"Somehow, your dumb ass stumbled into the wrong bar. You're in my MC's territory, and I don't like it," Navarro said. "Take your fat little partner and head back down to Mabel's."

"Fuck you," Whip snapped back. In a blur, his right hand swung toward Navarro.

Shit, he's got a knife.

Navarro lunged forward, blocked the attempted slash with his left forearm, and grabbed Whip's wrist with his right hand. In a split-second, the knife went flying across the floor. Some type of martial arts move followed, and Whip's body came crashing down to the floor.

Navarro's raised his right foot, then stomped down hard. With a gut-wrenching thud, the heel of his boot slammed into Whip's temple.

While Panda's hand nervously fumbled with the inside of his vest, Navarro punched him in the chest, which clearly knocked the air from his lungs completely. As he gasped for breath, the sound of a half-dozen lightning-fast punches hitting his face filled the bar.

With an almost elegant grace, Navarro flipped Panda over his shoulder, slamming him down onto the floor beside Whip.

The heel of his boot crashed down violently against Panda's skull.

After checking over his shoulder and making eye contact with me, he stomped each of their heads one more time. "Fucking idiots!" he shouted.

He picked up Whip's knife, and then took Panda's pistol.

I had no idea what type of military training Nicholas Navarro received, but whatever it was allowed him to singlehandedly pulverize two bikers in a matter of seconds. And, in doing so, he looked like a stunt man in a choreographed scene from an action-adventure movie.

I was scared, excited, and turned on at the same time.

Using Whip's knife, he carefully cut the patch from the back of each man's vest. After folding the patches up, he walked to the bar, then quickly returned.

He bent down and grabbed Whips ankles. "If that dumb fuck tries to get up, shoot him," he said over his shoulder.

"Will do, Nick," the bartender responded.

He dragged Whip through the door and into the parking lot.

In a few seconds, he returned and then dragged Panda outside.

He walked back in, and looked toward the bar. "Sorry about the burgers, Pete."

"No problem, Nick."

He turned toward me. "Come on," he said dryly. "We need to get."

I grabbed my purse. "Okay."

My heart was racing and my mind was trying to make sense of

everything that had happened. I wanted to ask so many questions, but realized the time had come for me to become more of a silent witness and less of an enthusiastic reporter.

Once we stepped into the parking lot, Navarro rushed to the semi-conscious men and planted the heel of his boot against their respective heads one more time.

Through his teeth he said his goodbyes. "Cocksuckers."

Silently, he started the motorcycle, put on his helmet, and turned to check on me.

"Hold on tight," he warned.

I nodded. "Okay."

"I've got to go see someone, and I don't have time to take you back."

"Okay."

"We're still off the record," he said. "Understand?"

"Fully," I responded.

Since I was a little girl, I'd always liked to collect facts and tell stories. A journalist was all I ever expected I would be. As sat in the parking lot with two half-dead bikers on the asphalt beside us, I was no longer a journalist working as a reporter for the newspaper.

I was an accomplice to aggravated battery.

I gripped Navarro's waist in my hands and waited. He revved the motor and released the clutch. The motorcycle sped out of the parking lot and into the street.

For that moment – and the moments that followed during that hot spring afternoon – I learned many things about Navarro.

And about myself.

TEN

NICK

One of the tell-tale signs of a promising prospect is his ability to realize when it's time to listen and when it's time to speak. A man who fully understands the difference without being told possesses a certain quality that evokes trust in the men who he exposes himself to.

Every passing moment of Peyton's silence pushed me closer to viewing her as a very intriguing woman, and not simply as the reporter who happened into the bar on that Friday afternoon.

We stood by the workbench in the shop while Peyton sat on my motorcycle in the parking lot. With my eyes constantly searching the road in front of the shop through the open garage doors, I conveyed my concerns.

"As far as I'm concerned we need to go to war with these pricks."

Pee Bee nodded. "I agree, Boss. If those two fucks came into Pete's bar, they were looking for what they got. That place is off-limits. Plenty of neutral places they could have caught up to you at, but they didn't. They were asking for it."

"Agreed."

"You sure you're ready for this?"

"Ready? If I'm breathing, I'm ready to fight. Don't forget that."

"Just askin', Crip. Just askin'."

"I'll call an emergency meeting," I said. "Let the fellas know to watch their backs. This could get real god damned ugly real god damned quick."

"What about the girl?"

I turned around and shot him a glare. "What about her?"

"Well, we got to do something with her. She ain't stickin' around for the meeting."

My stare continued, probably a little longer than it should have. For whatever reason, I now felt protective over her. I suspected it was a result of exposing her to the day-to-day life of an outlaw biker, and in doing so, placing her in harm's way.

His eyes widened. "Is she?"

"No," I snapped back. "She isn't sticking around for the fuckin' meeting. Her Jeep's at the coffee shop on Old Grove. I need to give her a ride back."

"Can't believe you got her to sit on that fuckin' fender. Don't know too many Ol' Ladies that'd ride on that fucker without a fight."

"She didn't have a choice."

"She's one tough little bitch," he said. "How'd she handle the beat down you gave Whip and Panda? Didn't barf or anything did she?"

"Handled it like a true professional." I chuckled. "When they showed up, I told her to stay in the booth. She sat there and watched me whip their asses. Little bitch never said a word. When we were walkin' out, I stomped both their fuckin' heads one more time, and she didn't say shit then, either. Never asked one fucking question."

He folded his arms in front of his chest and gazed in her direction. "Probably scared as hell."

"Her? Shit, I don't think so. She isn't a typical bitch. Said she snowboards, surfs, goes rock climbing, and bungie jumping. I doubt seeing me beat their asses scared her."

He rubbed his beard with his right hand and narrowed his eyes. "She interviewing you, or are you interviewing her?"

"She offered, I listened," I said. "Give me your keys."

He pressed his hands to his hips and shot me a look. "Say what?"

"Your keys to the bagger. Give 'em up. I'm taking her back to the coffee shop, and not on my Shovel."

He dug in his pocket, then handed me the keys. "Where's your key?"

"Ignition's hot all the time. Don't need a key."

"If you fuck her on it, clean up your mess," he said.

"If I fuck her on it, *she'll* clean up the mess."

"And make sure she doesn't drag her feet all over my fuckin' bags," he shouted as I walked away.

When I stepped to her side, she was still gazing out at the street.

"You alright?" I asked.

She turned around. "Yeah, why?"

"Just making sure."

"I was just thinking."

"About?"

"Learning to ride."

"You want a bike?"

She grinned and nodded. "Yep."

"Seriously?"

"Yep."

"You've never ridden before?"

"Nope."

"California's not a great place to learn. Traffic's a bitch."

HARD

"Corbet's Couloir in Jackson Hole, Wyoming is the most dangerous ski slope in the world. That's where I *learned* to snowboard. I surf at Black's Beach. There, you either ride the wave or eat a rock cliff. I don't do anything the easy way," she said.

"You'll probably love it," I said with a nod. "Hop off."

"Why?"

"We're not taking my bike." I motioned to Pee Bee's bike. "We're taking *that*."

"Why?"

I shrugged. "It'll be more comfortable for you. It's got air ride suspension, a CD player, and a gel-filled passenger seat. Hell, it's like riding a marshmallow down the highway."

"Not interested." She slapped the palm of her hand against the side of my gas tank. "I wanna ride on *this*."

I narrowed my eyes and fought the urge to smile. "Why?"

"Because this is a *real* bike," she said.

I exhaled, nodded, and walked back into the shop.

I tossed Pee Bee his keys. "Here."

"Not taking it?"

"She didn't want to ride on it."

He looked disappointed. "Why?"

"Said she wants to ride on a *real* bike."

"A real bike?"

I nodded. "Yep."

"Tell that skinny little bitch to go fuck herself," he said. "That *is* a real bike."

"Tell her yourself."

"I ain't walkin' all the way out there."

"I'm sure you'll be seeing her again," I said.

And I truly believed it.

ELEVEN

PEYTON

I learned to surf long before anything else. I wasn't quite a teenager at the time, and Phillip, my oldest brother, was seventeen. Preston was two years older than me, and two years younger than Phillip. With me being the youngest child – and the only girl – my father was slightly overprotective of me.

He took another gulp of his coffee and glanced at his watch. "You're too young."

"I'm almost thirteen."

"Like I said, you're too young."

"Phil started when he was ten."

"Phil's a boy. You're a girl. There's a difference."

"Is not."

"There is. And, I don't have time to argue. I'm almost late."

"I'm going," I said. "They're going to teach me."

It was summer, and we were out of school. With my father working, we had the entire ten-week period to ourselves. Our adventures were only limited by our imaginations and our courage, which were two things I seemed to have an overabundance of.

"They're most certainly not," he said. "Now I've got to go."

He leaned over and gave me a kiss. It was something he did every day before he left for work, but the level of affection didn't extend to my brothers. I didn't really think about it at the time, but as I got older, I came to believe he kissed me each day because I reminded him of mom.

And he missed her. Dearly.

She died when I was eight, the result of a multi-car pileup on the freeway. There were many cars that wrecked that day, but she was the only fatality. My father told me that she was far too beautiful of a woman to remain on earth, and that God recognized it and took her to heaven to be with the other angels.

I believed him.

It was difficult not to. My mother was a beautiful woman, and she was definitely an angel. Her skin resembled porcelain. Her hair was like silk, and her smile was infectious. She had a soft voice, her patience was never ending, and she always took the time to do whatever she must to keep us entertained.

"Maybe just a few lessons?"

He shook his head. "I don't want you to get hurt."

"I promise," I said, extending my pinkie. "I won't."

"You can't make that promise," he said.

I extended my arm and offered him my pinkie. "I just did."

"A few lessons, that's it." He sighed and reached for my hand. As our pinkies interlocked, he grinned. "Don't get hurt."

"Thanks, Dad."

I spent that entire summer surfing, and before school started, I was just as good as Phillip and Preston, which made neither of them very happy. Although most families took vacations in the summer, we took a different approach, vacationing during winter break.

While Phillip and Preston chose to downhill ski, I, being the more adventurous, learned to snowboard. By the time I was sixteen, I was an avid snowboarder. At eighteen, I was driving to Utah and climbing up the face of mountains where no one else had ventured.

People often asked if I had a death wish, or if I placed no value whatsoever on life. I always responded *no*, but never took time to explain.

In reality, my adventures took me to a place far away, somewhere between the heavens above and the earth below. With everything I did, be it surfing, snowboarding, or rock climbing, my feet were never planted firmly on the earth, and the euphoria I felt was heavenly.

Sometimes, so heaven-like, that I felt I could reach out and touch her hand.

To this day, I miss her dearly.

TWELVE

NICK

I glanced around the shop, taking time to make eye contact with each of the men. As they returned my gaze – some seeming eager, while others appeared concerned – I remained stone-faced.

"It's no secret that the Savages run thirty deep while our membership is eighteen. I don't say this for the sake of saying it. I say it because I believe it. Thirty deep or three hundred deep, it doesn't matter. There's not an MC on this earth that has more heart, soul, or guts than the Fuckers."

The shop erupted in fuck yeahs, grunts, and shouts. To boost morale, I gave the men a moment of celebration, then raised my hand and silenced the crowd. "It's no secret that this has been coming for some time, and ever since they stole Bunk's bike, they've been asking for it. Well, now they've decided it's okay to ride right into our territory, and even come into one of our bars. If we don't stand up now, ain't one of us worth the patches we're wearin'."

"What are we gonna do?" Stretch asked. "What's the plan?"

I nodded. "I'm getting' to that. We're not huntin' 'em down, but we're giving no grace when it comes to territory. Not now. If one of 'em is spotted on our turf, it's on. Right then and fucking there."

"If you whipped Whip's ass, you know they'll be comin' for us,"

Ryder said.

"*If* I whipped his ass? *If?* There's no if. I beat that motherfucker like he owed me money. And then I stomped his head in the dirt. Him and that little steroid eatin' sidekick of his, Panda. And, you're right. They'll be comin'. So, here's the best advice I can give each of you."

I raised my index finger in the air.

"If you're on your sled, you're going to be wearing your colors. If you're wearing your colors, you'll be a target. We need to always be in pairs." I pointed to Pee bee, and then to myself. "No exceptions. I realize there's going to be little short runs where you're alone, but what I'm talking about is being out *on the road* alone. Don't do it."

"Closest patch is ten miles from where I stay," Cholo said.

"Meet halfway. A ten-mile run alone on the highway is asking for it. I know some of you don't like doin' it, but splittin' lanes in this state is legal. If you get stuck in traffic, split lanes and get on down the highway."

I studied the men. Each of them stood in wait. Some for further instructions while others waited for reassurance that everything would be okay. A few probably hoped for an invitation to go bust someone's head.

"I know some of you are eager to bust heads, and there's others who would just as soon have this thing end without any bloodshed. Well, I got news for you, fellas. This won't come to an end without spillin' some blood. Not now. The Savages have gone too far this time. And if there's anyone thinking that what I did was wrong, go ahead and turn your patch in now. They came into our territory, walked into one of our bars, and pulled a knife on me. To tell the truth, if that reporter wouldn't have been with me, we'd probably be burying those two pricks"

"Where's it end?" Ryder asked.

"What do you mean?"

"Will this be like the Hells Angels and the Outlaws? A never ending battle that lasts a lifetime? If you say *no*, tell us what's going to stop it. What's gotta happen to get this thing to end?"

"Listen up, fellas," I shouted. "Ryder asked how this thing's gonna end? My answer isn't what any of you want to hear, but it's the best I've got. My answer's this: I've got no fucking idea. If these pricks give us the respect we deserve, then I guess it's over. If they don't, it'll continue until they do or they're all dead."

The men fell silent.

"Anyone take exception to what we're doing?"

Silence.

"Anyone want out of this club? Now's your chance. If you're not willing to be part of this, I'm going to ask you to turn in your patch. I'd rather have you walk away now than not have my back or one of the fellas backs when the shit gets real. And, believe me, it's gonna get real."

Silence.

"Nobody?"

"I've got somethin'," Pee Bee said.

"Listen up, fellas. Peeb's got something to say."

Pee Bee raked his fingers through his hair, glanced around the group, and sighed. Although I was the president of the club, the men looked at him as a spokesperson, their protector, and someone who would never bullshit them about club business.

"We might not follow society's rules, and we sure as fuck don't abide by society's laws. But, we've got a strict morale code that we live by. Our own set of rules. Each and every rule we follow gets back to the same thing, respect. We don't ride in San Bernardino County. Because we're pussies? No. Because we respect the Devil's Head MC. And we don't go to the Five Corners in Escondido. Why? It's a Hells Angels bar. We show respect to these clubs because we respect them. And, in return they give respect. What this is about, with the Savages, is respect. They don't respect us, and they're flexin' their muscles."

He raised his fist and flexed his bicep. "It's time we flex our muscles. We've got two of their patches in the safe. Far as I'm concerned, we ain't done 'till we got twenty-eight more. That's all I got. I'm droppin' my mic."

"Good point, Peeb." I nodded. "He's right, fellas. Respect. That's all we're asking for. And until they give it, we need to watch our backs."

Pee Bee's eyes shot wide and he motioned toward the street. "Fuck. Cops."

I turned toward the open garage doors. Without lights or sirens, police cruisers pulled in one after the other. After the fourth, an unmarked Dodge Charger parked alongside the last cruiser. In unison, eight uniform officers – and who I suspected were two detectives – got out of their cars at the same time.

The detective driving the unmarked charger stepped a few feet inside the shop and stopped. His partner and the remaining officers stood in position.

"Nicholas Navarro. You can either surrender, or we're coming in." He looked at his watch. "I'll give you fifteen seconds."

"Nobody do *anything*," I whispered. "Don't fucking move."

I took two steps forward, separating myself from the group of men. "I'm Nick Navarro. You placing me under arrest?"

He nodded. "I sure am."

"What are the charges?"

"You've got six seconds."

"What are the fucking charges?"

"The disappearance of Bryan Whipple for starters. Time's up."

I pulled off my kutte and handed it to Pee Bee. Having it confiscated by the police and used as a trophy during a news conference wasn't going to happen. After handing him my cell phone and wallet, I gave my only instruction. "Get the reporter to come see me in jail if they don't let me bond out."

"The girl?"

I nodded. "She works for the Union-Tribune. Name's Peyton Price. She'll be easy to find."

He folded the kutte over his forearm and nodded. "You got it, Crip."

I began walking toward the officers. After the third or fourth step, guns were drawn and commands were barked out as if I were a suicide bomber.

"Do not come any closer! Place your hands behind your head! Interlock your fingers, and lower yourself to the floor!"

Standing twenty feet from the officers, I locked eyes with big-mouthed detective. I slowly raised my hands, placed them behind my head, and interlocked my fingers.

"Get down on the floor!"

"I'm not getting on the floor."

"Get down on the floor!"

"I've got seventeen fucking witnesses. I'm not resisting arrest. I'm surrendering."

"Get down on the floor!" he shouted. "I'm not telling you again!"

HARD

No differently than the issues the MC was having with the Savages, I viewed the detective's demand that get on the floor as disrespectful. If I were resisting arrest, committing a crime, or attempting to evade arrest, I would have no other choice.

But I wasn't.

I was peacefully offering myself to them. His repeated commands were for no other reason than to feed his ego. I had little doubt that if it wasn't for the seventeen witnesses standing behind me, I would have been shot.

I shook my head. "I'm not telling *you* again. I'm surrendering without incident, *detective*."

He drew his weapon and pointed it at me. Nine others followed.

Sorry, fellas.

You're trying to scare the wrong man.

I'd been shot at far too many times to allow myself to become petrified by someone who was simply pointing a gun at me.

With his weapon pointed at my chest, he nodded his head toward the floor. "Get on the floor, or I'll shoot!"

I coughed out a laugh. "You got any idea how many of those fellas behind me have cell phones?"

His eyes thinned.

"And idea how many know how to push the *record* button?" I asked.

He exhaled heavily.

"I'm surrendering." I cleared my throat. "Now. Be a man, and come arrest me."

"Lower your weapons." He holstered his weapon and removed his handcuffs. "Turn around. Slowly."

I nodded. "Sure thing, *detective*."

I turned around, locked eyes with Pee Bee, and winked. He shook his head and grinned.

The detective frisked me, placed the cuffs on my wrists one at a time, and turned me to face the officers. "Nicholas Navarro, you are under arrest in association with the disappearance of Bryan Whipple. You have the right to remain silent. Anything you say can and will be used against you in a court of law. You have the right to an attorney. If you cannot afford an attorney, one will be provided for you."

"I'm under arrest?"

"You sure are."

"Under the protection afforded me by the Fifth Amendment of the US Constitution, I would like to exercise my right to remain silent. And, I refuse to subject myself to any questioning without having an attorney present," I said.

"So you're a gang member and a legal expert?" he asked in a sarcastic tone.

He was doing his best to goad me into a conversation, but it wasn't going to work. There were only two people I was going to talk to.

The club's attorney, and Peyton Price.

In that order.

THIRTEEN

PEYTON

I'd searched the house from one end to the other and couldn't find my recorder. I remembered having it at the coffee shop and placing it in my purse before we left, but now it was nowhere to be found.

Frustrated, I sat at my computer and began to type, using compiled notes from memory alone.

Although racism is commonly practiced by many similar clubs, the FFMC harbors no such beliefs, nor limits their membership by anything other than opinion. Navarro isn't a prejudiced man, and regardless of skin color, creed, or religious belief, if a man is capable of proving his worth to the club – an eighteen-month process – he may be voted in by a unanimous decision.

Somewhat of a flirt – and by his own admission a man who doesn't trust himself in the presence of women – Navarro's charisma arrives minutes before he does. Be it his confident swagger, his perfectly sculpted cheek bones, or his million-dollar smile, resisting his allure is no easy task.

His only means of transportation remains a vintage Harley-Davidson FLH, void of any options available in today's competitive motorcycle manufacturing market. While others in the club may ride custom baggers fitted with stereos, fairings, and hard saddle bags,

Navarro's personal selection must be kick-started.

I read what I had written and decided it was an acceptable place to start. Although I was initially eager to investigate and write the piece on Navarro's club, now that I had an opportunity to spend time with him, doing so seemed strangely out-of-place.

I highlighted everything and erased it.

Finding Nick Navarro attractive and *being* attracted to him were totally different. Any reasonably sane woman would find him attractive, but being attracted to him – especially after taking time to get to know him – would be foolish, or so I thought.

There was no real reason for me to be attracted to him.

But I was.

I felt my article not only needed to satisfy the expectations of my editor-in-chief, my readers, and myself, but Navarro as well. Leaving him out of the equation seemed irresponsible and insensitive.

And I was neither.

In a perfect world, I would have him sitting beside me while I wrote the article. Being certain to wear my glasses – and my shorts – I would tease him the entire time, leaving him no alternative other than to make sexual advances. Of course I would succumb to his wishes – all the while telling myself I was using him solely for my own personal satisfaction.

I was beginning to wonder if I was lying to myself.

As rough and impetuous as he was when it came to sex, I found his manner desirable in an almost infectious way. In his absence, I yearned for his forceful touch. In his presence, I anxiously waited for an opportunity to provoke him to exercise his lack of sexual control.

I recalled the exact moment his hand pressed my head into the surface of the workbench. I suspected most women would find such an act forceful and far from sensual. I, on the other hand, found it almost necessary.

At least now that I'd experienced it.

About the time I realized my daydreaming had made me horny beyond comprehension, the sound of a motorcycle's exhaust caused me to jump from my seat. I ran to my window, pulled the blinds, and was surprised to see Navarro's Sergeant-At-Arms pulling into the driveway of my townhome.

What the fuck?

I rushed to the door and yanked it open, fully expecting Navarro to be right behind him. After he shut off his rumbling motor, the silence that followed made my stomach curl into knots.

The look on his face confirmed my suspicion.

Something was wrong.

He removed his helmet, hung it on the handlebars, and tossed his leg over the gas tank. "Mind if I come in? We need to talk."

My mind started to race, and my throat went tight. "Yeah, uhhm. Come in."

***

We sat across from each other at my breakfast table, his face rather solemn and me on the verge of tears. I hadn't cried since my mother passed, and I found it almost haunting that Nick Navarro's arrest caused a baseball sized lump to rise in my throat and my eyes to well with tears.

"Do you know what the charges are?"

He nodded and cleared his throat. "They've charged him with everything they can. The attorney said it's pretty common. They charge him with everything in hope of him cutting a deal--"

"He won't, will he?"

He looked at me like I was insane. "Crip?"

Navarro's club name caught me off guard, and my response came slow. "Uhhm. Yeah, Crip."

"Fuck no. He'd die in there before he agreed to anything."

"So what are they? The charges? Can you tell me?"

He raised his right hand and extended individual fingers as he named each charge. "Breaking and entry, burglary, criminal mischief, theft, and suspicion of murder. There might be another, I can't remember."

Oh. My. God.

My immediate response wasn't one of wonder. *What happened* or *why* never came to mind. Doing any and everything in my power to assist in his release, however, did.

"What can I do to help?"

Thick strands of his long hair had fallen down into his eyes. He lowered his head, raked his fingers through it, and brushed it away from his face. "You got any beers around this place?"

It was late, and a drink sounded good. "Michelob Ultra. That's the only beer I have. Or you can have vodka and cranberry juice, which is what I'm going to have."

"No disrespect, but Michelob Ultra tastes like water. If I try one of them cranberry drinks, you ain't gonna tell Crip, are ya?"

"Not if you don't want me to."

He shot me his crazy-eyed stare. Again. "If I wanted you to tell him, I wouldn't have asked, would I?"

I grinned. "Probably not."

"Make me one of 'em, but make it like you were six-foot-eight and weighed two-sixty. You know, not for a girl."

"I don't drink like a girl, believe me."

I mixed two drinks, making them no differently than I would if I were drinking alone. I handed him one of them. "Are you really six foot eight?"

"Barefoot, yeah. In boots, six-ten and a little."

"Jesus."

"Tell me about it."

"Wow."

"Forty-inch inseam, size sixteen boots, and a double XL shirt. Try findin' shit that fits. Pain in the ass."

I took a drink. "Size sixteen? Seriously?"

He took a drink, swallowed, and then stared at the half-full glass. "Yep. And I know you're wonderin', so I'll just say it now. What they say *is* true. And no you can't see it."

I tried to keep from smiling. "I wasn't going to ask."

To be truthful, if I had a few drinks in me – and if I hadn't met Navarro – I would have asked.

"But you were wonderin'."

I took another drink. "We always wonder. It's part of being a girl."

He finished his drink and stared at the empty glass. "This fucker's good. And gone."

I extended my hand. "Let me make you another."

I mixed him another drink and handed it to him. "Here. And don't be shy. There's plenty. It's a staple here. Kind of like cottage cheese and yogurt."

He reached for the drink. "Thanks."

I sat down across from him and sighed. "So, back to what we were talking about. What can I do to help?"

"According to the attorney, you interviewed Crip on the 7th of May. For the first time. Now I ain't sayin' you did, and I ain't sayin' you didn't. I'm sayin' that's what the attorney said."

I didn't have to think about it. The date was stuck in my head. "I did. It was our first interview."

"The 7th was a Saturday."

I shook my head. "We started on a Sunday. Sunday night."

"Sunday was the 8th."

I grabbed my phone, opened the calendar, and stared at the dates. He was right. Saturday *was* the 7th and Sunday *was* the eighth. I had misspoken when the interview started. "Wow. Sunday was the 8th. We started on the 8th."

"Attorney said that Crip said you started the recording out by saying something like *this is Peyton Price and for the record, this is the 7th of May.* Crip remembers everything, especially when it comes to numbers."

He was right, I did say it, and I remembered saying it. His quote was almost verbatim. Confused as to what he wanted from me, I decided to just ask. "So, what does he need from me?"

"He needs you to say on the evening of the interview, you two were tied up until late. From whenever it started until late at night."

I shrugged. "We were."

He cocked an eyebrow. "And that the interview was on the 7th."

Apparently, Navarro needed an alibi. For whatever reason, I was ready to provide it. "I interviewed Navarro on the 7th. We started at roughly six o'clock, and the interview lasted until eleven p.m."

He shook his head. "It needs to last until 2:00 a.m."

"I interviewed Navarro on the 7th. We started at roughly six o' clock, and the interview lasted until 2:00 a.m."

He took a drink, then studied me for a moment. "They're gonna get rough with you in the interrogation room."

"I'm a big girl, I can handle it."

He cleared his throat. "You sure it was the 7th?"

"Positive."

He leaned forward and glared at me. "You're lying."

"Fuck you. I'm positive."

He wagged his finger in my face. "If I find out you're lying--"

I pushed myself away from the table and glared back at him. "You won't find out, shit, mister. I'm telling the truth. The interview started on Saturday, the 7th of May, and lasted until 2:00 a.m."

"How do you know it was the 7th?"

"Because it was on Saturday. And, I always start off my recordings with the date and the name of the interviewee."

"You got a copy of the recording?"

Fuck.

My recorder was lost.

"You don't need a copy of my recording, all you need is my testimony."

"I need a copy of that recording."

I stood up and crossed my arms in front of my chest. "Actually, you don't. Under oath, and facing the penalty of perjury, I have provided testimony. As a matter of law, testimony is a solemn statement or declaration of fact, and is a form of evidence in itself. Now, release Navarro or my next article will be a full front page on the corruption within the judicial system, and I'll start with my experiences here today with you, officer fucktard. Now, release Navarro or face the wrath of the

Union-Tribune."

He grinned. "One last question. How do you know it was 2:00 a.m.? Could it have been 1:00? Midnight? 1:30?"

"if you want the specific time, it was 2:06. Navarro and I had just finished speaking about a charity run he was trying to organize for orphaned children, and I looked at my watch. I recall saying, *holy shit, it's 2:06, I need to go.*"

He stood up. "I ain't sure what you and Crip got goin' on, so I ain't tryin' to get in the middle of that. And I ain't tryin' to be disrespectful either. But god damn, girl, you're the first bangin' ass hot bitch I ever met that's got her shit together. Most hot bitches are dumb as fuck."

I grinned. "Thanks."

He reached into his pocket, produced a tattered business card, and handed it to me. "I'm gonna get before you get me drunk. Give him a visit tomorrow. Call first. What you and I talked about? It didn't happen. When you talk to him, whatever you say--"

"I'll tell him the truth," I said. "That the interview was on the 7th, and that it ended at 2:06 a.m."

He clenched his fist and extended his arm.

I clenched mine and pounded it into his.

"Good lookin' out, Peyton Price," he said. "You get Crip out of jail, and I'll owe you. Big time."

"I'll hold you to it," I said.

He reached for his drink, and finished it in one gulp. "Good luck tomorrow."

"I don't need luck," I said. "I've got charm."

He grinned. "You've got *something*, that's for fuckin' sure."

He was right.

I was a thrill-seeking weirdo.

And lying to the cops to get Navarro out of jail was thrilling to me.

Now, all I needed to do was find an outfit to wear. And I needed to remember to wear my glasses.

FOURTEEN

NICK

I sat in my jail cell, wondering just how it was that a judge found it necessary to deny a bond hearing, claim me as a flight risk, and a modern-day terrorist on my native soil. My service to the nation was apparently all for naught, and my release from incarceration was dependent on the false testimony of a girl I didn't really know.

In club terms, *I was fucked*.

The sound of keys jingling warned me of a guard's approach. As the sound got closer and closer, I couldn't help but wonder if either Peyton decided to testify, or if they found DNA evidence of Whip's dead brother.

"Navarro! Hands to the door, I need to cuff you for court."

I had been placed in a maximum security cell, and unlike the majority of other men who were incarcerated in the jail, I wasn't free to roam. I turned around, backed up to the door, and placed my wrists in front of the hinged opening in the steel door.

Within a few seconds, my hands were cuffed. A few seconds later, and I was fitted with a waist chain and shackles.

I walked in a few steps in front of the guard, well aware of the route we were taking to get to the courtroom. Upon entering the room, however, I was pleasantly surprised to see Peyton, dressed in a black skirt, white shirt, and black blazer.

Her conservative heels topped off the ensemble, but it was her glasses that commanded my attention.

You wore those on purpose, didn't you?

Almost immediately after being seated beside Tristan Beecham, the club's attorney, the judge entered the courtroom.

"All rise," the bailiff said.

Although she was seated twenty feet from me, the smell of Peyton's shampoo and perfume caused my mouth to water.

The judge sat down.

"You may be seated."

The judge shuffled through a stack of paperwork, picked up a sheet of paper, and studied it. After a moment, he placed the paper down on his desk and raised his head. "In the matter of the people versus Nicholas Navarro, new testimony has been given which corroborates previous testimony given by the accused, and supports statements regarding the whereabouts of the accused on the night in question. The witness has agreed to testify before me, which I require in any such case."

"Mrs. Price, will you approach the witness stand?"

Peyton stood. "Yes, Sir."

She gracefully walked to the witness stand.

"Raise your right hand."

She did.

"State your name."

"Peyton Penelope Price."

"Mrs. Price, do you swear – or affirm – that the testimony you give here today is the truth, the entire truth, and nothing but the truth?"

"I do."

"Have a seat, please."

Peyton sat in the witness stand. The judge nodded toward the prosecutor's bench. "Your witness."

"Mrs. Price. I haven't had an opportunity to hear your testimony, but it's been brought to my attention that you gave testimony today in the presence of two detectives regarding the whereabouts of one Nicholas Navarro on the night in question. Is that correct?"

"I have no idea," she responded.

"Excuse me? Can you speak up?"

She leaned forward and spoke into the microphone. "I have no idea."

"You have no idea? Regarding what, Mrs. Price?"

She cleared her throat. "You stated that I gave testimony to two detectives regarding the whereabouts of one Nicholas Navarro on the night in question. My response is this: I have no idea when the *night in question* is. I gave testimony regarding Mr. Navarro's whereabouts on the night that he was involved in an interview with me. If the night of the interview and the *night in question* correspond with one another, I suppose you have your answer, Sir."

"On the night of May 7th, did you interview Nicholas Navarro?"

"Yes, Sir. I did."

"What is your profession, Mrs. Price?"

"I'm a journalist, employed by the Union-Tribune, as a reporter."

"On that night, when did the interview start?"

"6:00 p.m."

"Are you certain?"

"I'm positive. If I weren't, I wouldn't testify, Sir."

The prosecutor nodded. "I appreciate that, ma'am."

"And when, Mrs. Price, did the interview end?"

"2:06 a.m., Sir."

Thank you.

"2:06, huh? Are you certain it was 2:06?"

"Yes, Sir. Again, if I wasn't, I wouldn't provide testimony regarding a specific time."

"How, Mrs. Price, are you so certain of the time?"

"I checked my watch immediately prior to ending the meeting. I recall saying, it's 2:06 a.m., I need to go."

"2:06 on the 7th?"

"No, Sir."

"It wasn't the 7th?"

"When it ended, Sir, it was the 8th. It was after midnight."

"At any time during the interview, did Mr. Navarro leave your sight?"

"No, Sir, he did not."

"Not once?"

"No, Sir."

"Are you certain?"

"Quite."

"So, you interviewed Mr. Navarro for eight hours?"

"That is correct."

"At any point in time did you or Mr. Navarro eat?"

"No."

"Drink?"

"Yes."

"Did you or Mr. Navarro take an opportunity to urinate?"

"Yes, as a matter of fact, we did."

The prosecutor chuckled. "Did you assist him?"

"No, I did not."

"So, he did leave your sight?"

"No, he did not."

The prosecutor shook his head. "Can you explain?"

"Sure. I interviewed Mr. Navarro in the equivalent of an abandoned warehouse. Mr. Navarro and I, on the evening and night that we're speaking of, consumed drinks. At one point, Mr. Navarro stated that he *needed to piss.* I informed him that I needed to as well, and asked the way to the bathroom. He laughed and said the building did not have a working bathroom, but that it was in the process of being repaired. I then asked where he intended to urinate. He pointed to the parking lot. I chose to hold it, and he chose not to. While he urinated, Sir, I stood in the building and watched."

Where the hell did that story come from?

The prosecutor sighed. "No further questions."

The judge cleared his throat. "Mrs. Price, do you understand that it is a crime for providing false testimony?"

"Yes, Sir, I do."

"The crime of perjury."

"Yes, Sir, I understand."

"And, you understand you're under oath to tell the truth?"

"Yes, Sir, I do."

The judge nodded. "Will the accused please rise?"

Beecham and I both stood.

"Mr. Navarro, testimony has been provided that corroborates your claim, and provides you with an alibi on the night in question. Regarding the fingerprint on the fuel tank of the motorcycle, we must assume that was left at a date prior to the victim's disappearance. For the mix-up, the court apologizes. You are free to go."

I nodded. "Thank you, your honor."

"Have you any questions, son?"

"None, your honor."

"Be it a matter of record, that in the matter of the people versus Nicholas Navarro, the charges, in their entirety, have been dismissed."

The judge stood.

"Please rise," the bailiff bellowed.

The judge left the room.

"You may be seated, and you're dismissed," the bailiff stated.

The sheriff's officer walked to the bench, unlocked my cuffs, and removed the shackles.

"Any questions?" Beecham asked.

"Nope," I said.

"I'll send you a bill."

Out of the corner of my eye, I noticed Peyton walking toward the door. I felt like yelling at her, telling her to stop, and asking to use her cell phone, but realized I had to refrain from any contact with her – at least in the courtroom.

Not telling her how much I appreciated her help was difficult. Having no idea if she was going to remain the same person toward me after she gave her testimony was worse. The possibility of losing whatever it was we shared sank into the pit my stomach like a rock.

It was painfully obvious she meant more to me than some girl who was simply interviewing me.

I liked the thought of it.

But I wasn't sure if I could allow it.

FIFTEEN

PEYTON

I ran down the hallway and ducked into my office. After retrieving my laptop, I turned around and attempted to run out of the building without being seen. I was mere inches from the door, and the sound of Camden Rollins' booming voice made the hair on the back of my neck stand up.

"Peyton! What in the world are you doing?"

Fucking fuck fuck fuck.

With my laptop clutched under my right arm, and my purse dangling under my left, I turned around and forced myself to smile. "Just came in to get my MacBook. It's has some stuff on it that I need to make reference to."

He crossed his arms and stared back at me in disbelief. "Were you running?"

"It uhhm. It was. It was more of a light jog."

"Why are you in such a hurry?"

I shrugged. "Just. I uhhm. Trying to get done with the first installment of an awe-inspiring piece."

"Come on back." He turned away. "I haven't seen you in weeks."

"Has it been weeks?" I asked. "It seems like hours."

"Come on back," he said over his shoulder. "You can bring me up to speed."

"I really need to try and get this done before I have a brain fart."

He didn't respond.

I took a few backward steps, inching closer to the door. "I uhhm. My recorder. I lost my voice recorder. Misplaced is more like it. But I figured out where I left it. Or at least I think I did. I was having lunch with Navarro. Kind of. Well, we never actually ate, but that's an entirely different story. Anyway, I'm thinking I'll have a rough draft here pretty soon."

He walked away from me, reached the end of the hallway, and disappeared around the corner. I glanced at the receptionist. She returned an innocent smile and shrugged.

"Thanks for the warning," I whispered.

I sighed, placed my MacBook on the receptionist's desk, and took off in a dead run toward his office. When I reached the door, I reluctantly pushed it open. "I really need to go. I need to get my recorder. I left it at the bar."

He waved his hand toward the front side of his desk. "They'll be open all day. Have a seat, Peyton."

I sighed and flopped down in the chair.

"What's on your laptop that's so important?" he asked.

"Just stuff."

"What kind of stuff? Must be pretty important if you're rushing in here to get it in the middle of the day. And why are you dressed like that? The Filthy Fuckers will never trust you if you're dressed like that."

I was still wearing my outfit from testifying in court. "No, I had a meeting. I uhhm. My insurance company. New insurance. They were going to cancel me. Too many tickets."

"You need to slow down. You drive like a maniac. How many times have I told you? You need to slow down. You're going to end up--" He paused, swallowed and shook his head. "You need to slow down."

I nodded. "Duly noted."

"So, what was it you were after? Tell me about the Filthy Fuckers. Are they going to war with Satan's Savages?"

I sat up straight. "I was wanting to look at some notes from a few years ago I was chasing that missing person's case."

"Suspect the MC for a murder?"

"No. No." I shook my head and forced a laugh. "Not even close. I was just wanting to look at some things. Unrelated. Kind of."

"What about Satan's Savages? Heard anything?"

"Not a word," I said. "Interesting bunch, though. The Fuckers, that is. It'll be a great piece."

"We won't be able to give the piece away if there isn't any action. MC's are a dime a dozen if they're riding up and down the PCH swilling beers and getting in fist fights."

"You'll be pleased. I promise."

He fixed his eyes on me and rubbed his chin between his thumb and forefinger. After a moment, he relaxed in his seat. "Alright. Go get your recorder. Dig deep, Peyton. I know you've got it in you."

I inhaled a deep breath and prepared to stand.

"Before you go, what about Navarro? He's a mean son-of-a-bitch from what they say. Have you had a chance to spend some time with him?"

I sighed. "Uhhm, yeah. I mean, the spending time with. Not as much as I need to, though."

"Is he as hot-tempered as they say?"

I stood up and shrugged. "I sure haven't seen it. Not yet."

HARD

He picked a pencil up from his desk and wagged it at me. "Dig deep. That's my advice. The deeper, the better."

"Will do, Sir." I said with a nod. "It'll go deep. I mean I'll go deep."

"Keep me posted," he said.

During the lull in conversation, I made my way to the door. "Will do."

No response.

I walked out the door, stepped into the hallway, and as soon as I was out of sight, took off running.

A case I was working on two years' prior shared almost all of the characteristics of Navarro's case. Whether or not Navarro was involved with either case was irrelevant, I simply wanted to know if the charges against him were according to state statutes, and if they could re-charge him at a later date.

I picked up the laptop, shot the receptionist a scowl, and ran to my Jeep.

One more stop, and then I could see if Navarro was out of jail yet.

***

I pulled into the parking lot of the bar, which was empty. From what Navarro said, the bar was a biker hangout, and his club had claimed it as their own. Although other people may frequent the bar, there was no worry of another MC stepping into FFMC's turf, which made the bar safe – at least for me.

I shouldered my laptop and walked inside. Pete stood behind the bar staring at the wall-mounted television in the distance.

He turned toward me and nodded his greeting. I nodded in return.

After scanning the bar for patrons and finding none, I walked to the bar. Pete's focus shifted from the T.V. to me. He resembled Navarro, but was smaller in stature, and missing the tattoos.

"I was in the other day with Crip." I motioned toward the area where the incident went down with Panda and Whip. "I think I might have left something--"

He raised his hand. "Looking for this?"

"Yes. Oh my God, that's great."

I slapped my hand against the carrying case for my laptop. "Mind if I sit over there and look for something on this?"

"Take all the time you need."

"Do you have wi-fi?"

He nodded. "Sure do. Password's *go home*."

I laughed. "Cute. Uhhm. Can I get. Can I get a Budweiser?"

I reached for my purse. He looked at me like paying was an insult. "On the house."

"Let me just--"

"It's on the house."

I raised the bottle. "Thank you."

I sat down at the same table Navarro and I had shared a few days prior. After logging onto the wi-fi, I began sipping my beer and searching through the documents of my old case. In no time, I was buried in legal facts and needed another beer.

The unmistakable sound of approaching motorcycles made my heart race. Expecting Navarro, Pee Bee and maybe more, I tore my eyes away from my laptop and peered through the window.

Much to my surprise, Whip, Panda, and several other Savages pulled into the parking lot.

Fuck.

My eyes shot toward Pete. I felt the need to warn him, just like Navarro did. "Savages coming in," I shouted.

He shifted his eyes toward the back door. "Go out the back."

I shook my head and reached for my recorder. "I'm staying."

I was almost sick from the excitement. I turned on my recorder, wedged it between the cushions of the booth's seat, and then slumped in my seat.

Whip, Panda, and two others came through the door and walked directly toward the bar.

"You got some of our shit," Whip growled. "And we need it back."

"I'll give it to you when go, and you need to go." Pete pointed toward the door. "Now."

"We'll leave when we're good and god damned ready," Whip responded. "Give me our shit."

I considered getting my phone and after sending Navarro a text message, recording video of the debacle. So far, I had gone unnoticed, and drawing attention to myself was the only thing that prevented it.

Standing directly in front of Pete, but on the other side of the bar, Whip checked over each shoulder, and without any further warning, thrust his head into Pete's face. Instantly, blood burst from Pete's nose. After Whip threw a few sucker punches, he climbed over the bar and began to rummage around.

While he did, one of the other bikers – a tall lanky man with long strands of filthy hair – scanned the bar. Upon seeing me, our eyes locked.

Fuck, fuck, fuck.

Whip handed Panda his pistol and then a shotgun, which I suspected was what Pete used to protect the bar. My heart sank at the thought of

Pete not being able to defend himself – or me for that matter – from the Savages.

The lanky biker pointed toward me. "See this?"

Whip's eyes met mine. "I'll be god damned. That's Crip's girl. The one that lied in court this morning."

Please. Let me live through this.

That's all I ask. Don't let them kill me.

Let me tell this story.

He shoved his knife into his pocket and began walking toward me. Two of the other three men followed.

I considered doing a lot of things, but only managed to do one. I turned toward him, blocking my right arm from his view. And, like a true journalist, I swept my purse and the recorder onto the floor. My only hope was that he didn't find them, leaving the recorder to capture the event in its entirety.

I stood up. "He's on his way. We're meeting here."

It was all I could think of, and was well worth a try.

He stepped directly in front of me, stopped, and eyes me from head to toe. "Better get this over with before he shows up."

Before I could react, he grabbed a fistful of my hair and yanked me to his side. A sharp pain shot through my scalp and along my spine.

I looked down, saw the toe of his boot, and stomped my heel into it as hard as I could.

He spun me around. "You little bitch," he seethed.

His hand slammed against my face. It wasn't a slap. Not even close. He hit me.

With his fist.

I stumbled, but didn't fall. "He's gonna kill you," I said through my teeth.

He pulled off my blazer, ripped my shirt, and pulled my bra up over my boobs. I fought against him at first, but it did little good.

His hand shot up my skirt and ripped off my panties.

"Don't you dare rape me," I said clearly and concisely.

I wanted the recorder to catch every word.

"Shut the fuck up. We're all gonna get some of you, you lying little whore."

He shoved me against the booth, bent me over, and pulled my skirt over my hips.

I refused to become a victim. Shedding a single tear wasn't an option. While the sound of the other men's voices either cheered him on or claimed their place in line, I felt his filthy skin against mine. The smell of gasoline, beer, and filth filled my nostrils, and I fought not to vomit.

I bit my lower lip and closed my eyes. I mentally struggled with him, the other, and what – if anything – I could do. Eventually, my mind gave up and drifted away.

While he pounded himself into me, my body may have been in the bar with him, but my mind and spirit were far away.

On a ski slope in Wyoming.

So high I could almost touch the clouds.

SIXTEEN

NICK

Sitting in jail wasn't something I ever yearned for. Each time it happened, however, it caused me to appreciate the small things in my life that I had been taking for granted. It seemed having them stripped away – along with my freedom – was a bit of a reality check.

"So she didn't even hesitate?" I asked.

"I'm fuckin' tellin' ya." Pee Bee grinned and shook his head. "She just kinda volunteered."

I shook my head. "She's a good woman."

"Best one I ever met. Smart bitch, too. She was tellin' me about laws and what they could and couldn't do to you. I'm tellin' ya, she's got her shit wired tight."

I leaned against the work bench. "I'm thinking about taking her to dinner. Doing something nice with her. Letting her know how much I appreciate it."

I didn't need Peeb's approval, but I wanted it. I took a drink of beer and waited.

"You should probably take her to dinner and then throw her some dick. Maybe instead of fuckin' her in the shop, you should do it at your house."

I chuckled. "You think dicking her at the shop's a bad idea?"

He shook his head. "Givin' her some cock in the shop ain't no big deal, Crip. But chicks want dicked on somethin' soft every now and again."

"On something soft?"

He finished his beer and got another from the fridge. "A bed, in the yard, on the couch. Hell, even in the back seat of a car. They like it. Take her out to eat and then give her some cock on somethin' squishy."

"Something squishy." I laughed. "I'll look into that."

Pee Bee – which stood for Pretty Boy – was a former USC football player. Although he had a college education, one would never really know it from talking to him. It was obvious that the mainstream idea of an education was not what he walked away with during his tenure as a student.

His heart was huge, his devotion to the club was undeniable, and he was – if anyone was – my best friend. He was a very handsome man. So handsome, that immediately following college he was chosen to be on a reality television show.

From time-to-time, he was recognized by someone in a bar – generally a woman. The conversations seemed to always start with *do I know you from somewhere*, and ended with Pee Bee balls-deep in yet another stranger.

Obtaining his advice on what women wanted seemed out of place. But he was one of the few men I trusted.

His eyes dropped to his boots for a moment. After some thought, he met my gaze. "I need to do somethin' for her too, just haven't decided what."

"Why's that?"

"Told her if she got you out of jail, I owed her one. A big one."

"Well, aren't you fuckin' sweet." I said sarcastically. "Just remember--"

I paused, and tried to decide whether or not to continue my thought. Before I had a chance to do so, he read my mind.

"I ain't gonna touch her."

I nodded. "Last fuckin' thing I need is some split-tail hangin' around. She's uhhm. She's pretty entertaining, though."

My phone beeped, indicating a text message had been received. Although I had a phone, I never really used it, nor did I have a desire to. If someone was sending me a text message, it was generally regarding being late for a meeting.

With no meeting scheduled, I was left believing the text must have been from Peyton.

Eager to see what she wanted, I grabbed my phone. After opening the text message screen, I saw one unread message.

But it wasn't from Peyton.

It was from Pete.

Sabages got thr girl htfu bring forepower. Whip here now Sorry they got my gun

"Motherfuckers!" I screamed. "God fucking fuck…"

"What?"

"I'm gonna kill…I'm going to kill *all* those motherfuckers!" I kicked the bench, sending shit flying everywhere.

My vision blurred, my ears started to ring, and I began to shake. "Fuuuuuuuuck!"

"What?" Pee Bee shouted.

I'd brought her into a world that she had no business in, and if something happened to her, it was on my shoulders.

HARD

I fought against the rising lump in my throat and tried to swallow, but couldn't. I turned toward the safe. While I poked the tip of my finger against the keypad, I tried to explain the text to Pee Bee.

"Text's from Pete. Can't tell for sure, but it looks like the Savages are at Pete's bar. They've got Pete's gun, and they've--"

I swallowed heavily, pulled the door of the safe open, and grabbed two pistols – one of which was fitted with a silencer.

I pursed my lips and inhaled a long breath through my nose. My hands began to shake. "They've got the reporter."

"Motherfuckers." He grabbed the silenced pistol. "If they even touch her, I'll kill the whole fucking club."

You'll have to beat me to it, Brother.

SEVENTEEN

PEYTON

More than anything, I wanted to scrub myself with soap and water. I needed the filth washed away. All of it. I feared I would never be clean again, regardless of how hard I scrubbed.

"Let me call an ambulance," Pete said. "Please. You need…you need to be checked out."

I fastened my bra and tried desperately to button my shirt, but there were no buttons. My eyes dropped to the floor. Scattered about, the small pieces of faux shell littered the floor surrounding the booth.

"I'm okay." I rubbed my hand against my swollen lip. "I'll *be* okay."

I knelt down, picked them up, and stood. I gazed blankly into the palm of my hand, wishing they were where they belonged. I noticed my torn panties on the bench where Navarro and I had been sitting just days before.

I clutched the broken buttons and reached for my panties. "Do you have a trash can?"

He nodded. "There's one by the bar."

I walked to the trash can and dropped my panties inside. When I returned, I crawled under the table and retrieved my purse. After dropping the broken buttons inside, I grabbed the recorder and turned it off.

HARD

"You're in shock," Pete said.

"No. I'm okay, really." I wanted to rewind the recorder and make sure it recorded everything, but I wasn't ready to listen to it. Not yet.

The sound of a motorcycle's exhaust caused me to flinch. It seemed something I had yearned to hear only hours before had somehow become repulsive, and I didn't like it. I peered out the window just in time to see Navarro and Pee Bee pulling up to the front of the bar.

"Navarro's here. I uhhm." I tugged against the sides of my shirt, attempting –to pull them together, but couldn't. I held the two pieces of material, concealing my bra from sight, and then remembered I had worn a blazer.

I searched the floor, found my jacket, and slipped my arms through it. Remarkably, it was unharmed. Methodically, I fastened the buttons, yet still felt slightly undressed when I was finished.

I brushed the lint from my skirt and tossed my hair. "No ambulance. I'll be fine. I need a drink. Maybe get us three beers?"

Navarro and Pee Bee came rushing in. Pete turned toward the door and met them halfway. Navarro ran past him, and came where I was standing. Pee Bee stood at Pete's side and talked to him while Navarro looked me over.

I gazed at him, rocking back and forth on the balls of my feet, and then realized I didn't have my heels.

He pressed his hands against my shoulders and held me steady. "What happened?"

I wished I didn't have to tell him. Sooner or later he'd find out for sure, but I just didn't want to have to talk about it. Not to him.

"Peyton," he squeezed my shoulders in his hands. "What happened?"

"Four of them. Whip, Panda, Lowbrow and Taffy. They uhhm." My eyes began to well with tears. I pointed to the portion of my shirt that the blazer didn't cover. I fought to swallow, eventually did, and continued. "They…"

I pointed to the trash can. "I put my panties in the trash."

He pulled me into his chest and held me tight. "I'm sorry. Believe me, they'll…I'll make sure that they…" His voice faltered, then he cleared his throat. "Did Pete call an ambulance?"

"I don't need one."

He looked into my eyes. "You need to see a doctor."

I nodded. "I will. I'll get checked out. But I'm not calling the police. I don't want them involved. I want…"

I wanted to tell him to take care of it, but couldn't put the responsibility on him to do so. I wished he would volunteer, and explain to me in detail how he would make them pay for what they did to me.

Pee Bee walked to Navarro's side, inhaled a deep breath, and exhaled into the palms of his hands. "Pete said it was Whip, Panda, Taffy, and someone else, but he wasn't sure."

"Lowbrow," I said flatly.

"You sure?"

I nodded. "Positive."

"Already called Ryder," he said. "Cholo and a bunch of the fellas were at his place. They're on their way now. You stay here with her."

Navarro released me and turned to face Pee Bee. "I'm going. I'm gonna kill every motherfucking one of 'em. Real god damned slow."

Pee Bee shook his head. "Somebody's got to stay with her."

"This is my fight, god damn it. Mine," Navarro seethed. "And I'm gonna fight it."

"You want him to stay?" Pee Bee asked. "Here with you?"

I nodded. "Uh huh."

"You don't want him to leave?"

I wrapped my arms around Navarro and pulled him into me. "I'd rather he stay, please."

Pee Bee folded his massive arms on front of his chest and sighed. "I'm the Sergeant-At-Arms of this club. It's my job to protect what's ours, at any cost. Like it or not, she testified for you, and this is the price she's paid for it. The club owes her. The club needs to protect her. I'm goin' for these motherfuckers, and I ain't stoppin' till I got 'em." He turned around until his back faced us. "Either let me get 'em, or cut off my fuckin' patch."

Oh, wow.

"You know good and god damned well I'm not cuttin' off your patch," Navarro growled.

"It's settled, then. You're stayin', and I'm goin'."

Navarro leaned over and rested his head on my shoulder. His warm breath on my neck made me smile. His strong arms provided assurance that I was safe from harm as long as he was near.

"I want 'em to pay."

Pee Bee nodded. "They will."

"Be careful," I said. "Panda's got a gun."

He laughed a dry laugh. "Me? Shit. Make me up one of those cranberry drinks. A double. I'll be over to drink it before the fuckin' ice melts."

I lifted my head. "Promise?"

A thunderous rumble rattled the windows of the bar. The sound continued for some time, almost resembling a passing train. I peered outside. Side-by-side, motorcycles pulled into the lot, one row after another. A string of headlights as far as I could see filled the road leading to the bar. It seemed it was never going to end.

In no time, the lot was filled with bikes.

Completely filled.

And, it wasn't just FFMC's men.

Pee Bee bent down, looked through the window, then stood up. "We're gonna roll, Boss."

Navarro cleared his throat. "Who else you call?"

"*Hell On Earth* and *The Dragons*. We're rolling about fifty deep, Boss."

"God damn you," Navarro said with a laugh. "We didn't need to--"

"You want my job?" Pee Bee interrupted. "Start wearin' my patch. Until you do, you be the President. I'll be the Sergeant-At-Arms."

The door opened and twenty or so men came in, all wearing leather vests. Two massive men came to our side and stood, each crossing their arms in front of their chests as they positioned themselves beside us.

"What's shakin', motherfuckers?" Pee Bee asked.

Each of the men hugged Pee Bee and patted him on the back. "Good to see you, Brother," one said.

"Tiny." Navarro nodded to the man on the left. "Big Frank," he said to the other.

"Crip," they said in unison.

Pee Bee turned toward the door.

"Pee Bee," I shouted.

He turned around.

"Promise me you'll be careful?"

He turned around, clenched his fist, and extended his arm.

I pounded my fist into his. "I'll have that drink waiting."

HARD

He walked away, and Navarro held me in his arms. As the walls and windows once again began to shake, I watched them leave. Two at a time, fifty motorcycle's taillights rode away from the bar and into the street. Each stood as a reminder that someone was going to pay dearly for what happened to me.

But nothing would ever be enough.

EIGHTEEN

PEE BEE

It was darker than a motherfucker in Whip's kitchen, but there I sat, waiting for his dumb ass to come home. Sooner or later I knew he would, even if it was just to get some stuff for the road. With the silenced pistol in my lap, and a straight razor in my pocket, I was ready to give him exactly what the other three men got, which was much less than what he deserved.

The life of a one-percenter is an interesting life to live. Sometimes years pass, and it's nothing but breathing in and breathing out. Then, something happens, and each day is like a trip through a booby-trapped minefield – one carefully placed step after another.

Without having some kind of laws in effect, society would be in utter turmoil. In a world without strict rules and regulations, it would stand to reason that the strong would survive, and the weak would perish, but I'm not convinced that's actually the case.

At least not in the world I live in.

Outlaws live beyond the limits of conventional law, most abiding to a strict set of moral codes and standards that prevent the complete collapse of the world they live in. Outside the world of the outlaw, two types of people live.

Law abiding civilians, and the lawless. One adheres to society's standards. To the other, there are no rules.

The lawless prey on any and everything that will provide them with a means to fuel their unrestricted life for one more day, never caring who or what they harm in the process.

The lawless have one concern.

Themselves.

The faint sound of a motorcycle exhaust shook me from what was soon to be a light sleep. I glanced at my watch.

3:30 a.m.

As the sound grew closer, I stood up, stretched, and checked the breech of the pistol. I'd checked it half a dozen times before, but doing it was from force of habit.

The garage opener activated, and I grinned to myself. One way or another, satisfaction was going to come. Hidden behind the doorway that led into the kitchen, I could see into the living room, but it would be almost impossible for anyone entering from the direction of the garage to see me.

I lowered myself to the floor, pointed the pistol toward the living room, and waited.

I heard the bike pull up. The garage door closed, and then the door to the house opened. In the complete silence, the sound of the creaking floor warned me of his arrival. With each step that he took, I held my breath and waited.

As his silhouette passed into my line of sight, I steadied my gloved fingertip against the trigger.

"What's shakin', motherfucker?" I asked.

He gasped and jumped to the side, still uncertain of where I was.

"Raise both your hands in the air right now, or I'll drop you where you fuckin' stand."

The little bit of light that seeped in through the blinds illuminated him enough that I could see the expression on his face. Concerned, and still unsure of my exact whereabouts, his eyes narrowed. He scanned the perimeter of the living room for a glimpse of me.

But his hands didn't immediately go up.

I pointed the pistol at his left thigh and pulled the trigger. The sound from the silenced .45 caliber pistol was about as loud as a can of beer being opened. The screaming that followed was deafening.

He fell to the floor.

I stood up.

Over the sound of his wailing and crying, I gave my only demand. "Keep your hands where I can see 'em, or I'll put one in your other leg."

His arms shot out to his sides.

"I need…a…I need a tourniquet. I'm gonna bleed…bleed to death."

I pointed the pistol at his other leg and pulled the trigger. "Shut the fuck up."

He screamed and clutched his thigh in his hands.

I had experience at making gunshot wounds, but I had no experience regarding the *treatment* of gunshot wounds. I had no idea if he would bleed to death or not. I'd read enough articles over the years about random shootings to know that gunshot victims often lived for hours before reaching a hospital.

To be honest, I prefer that he live, especially in the state I was going to leave him.

When he and his three club brothers showed up at the hospital with the same exact wounds, police would assume – rightfully so – that revenge had been sought out for a crime committed against another club.

But the Savages wouldn't say a word about who did it. A combination of embarrassment and a hatred for law enforcement would prevent them from it.

The one and only constant shared between the lawless and the outlaw was that snitching to the police didn't happen.

Resolution was obtained from within the ranks. It was a matter of honor.

I pushed the pistol into my front pocket, unbuckled his belt, and pulled up on the buckle end. After lifting him off of the floor by the belt, the wide leather slipped through his belt loops one by one, until it was finally free.

"I guess I'll wrap this fucker around the first one I shot."

"Just call me an ambulance, brother. I won't say a word."

"Brother? We're brothers now? You dumb fuck. You don't have a clue, you know it? I'm just gettin' started."

While he moaned and bitched, I wrapped the belt around his left thigh and pulled it tight. I then reached for the button of his jeans.

Whip wasn't as big as me, but he was a big man. As soon as I attempted to unbutton his pants, he knew what was next, and the struggle began. A few seconds into it, and I stood and pulled the pistol from my pocket.

I pointed it at his head.

"Tell you the truth, I don't care. We decided not to kill you pricks in a vote, but I'll let you pick. Either lay still or I'll put one in your head."

"Fuck you."

If it worked on your brother, it ought to work on you.

I kicked him in the side of the head as hard as I could.

Now on the floor unconscious, he provided no resistance. After putting the pistol in my pocket, I bent down, unfastened his pants, and pulled them to his thighs.

I reached in my back pocket, pulled out the straight razor, and grabbed his nuts with my gloved hand. I had visions of talking mad shit to him while I did the deed, but with him unconscious, it made the experience much less enjoyable.

I pulled down on his scrotum, stretched it tight, and swung the straight razor directly under the base of his cock. The entire wad of flesh came off in my hand, nuts and all.

"Holy fucking shit, that's nasty."

He began to stir around. Instead of listening to him, I kicked him in the head again.

Now, the really gross part.

It's a good thing I'm wearing rubber gloves.

I gripped the tip of his cock between my left thumb and forefinger, pulled up on it as hard as I could, and stretched it to its limit. As he began to writhe around, I swung the razor into the flesh and cut it almost all the way through.

"This motherfucker's dull as fuck," I said. "Makes sense, I've been through three cocks tonight. Four, now."

About the time he opened his eyes, I swung the razor into the little flap of flesh that still remained. His entire cock came off in my hand.

"Holy shit. That's a lot of blood."

He screamed out in pain and shoved his hands between his legs, no doubt in shock from what had happened.

"Well, Whip. You won't be raping any more girls with this, because I'm gonna take it with me."

I reached into my kutte, pulled out the Zip-Lock bag, and unzipped it. After dropping his cock and scrotum into the bag, I squeezed the air out, zipped it closed, and folded it up.

Whip would spend the rest of his life – if he lived through the gunshot wounds and the castration – without having sex again.

Not a day would pass that he wouldn't regret what he did to Peyton.

A life of pain, agony, humiliation, and regret.

But it would never be enough.

***

Crip's door opened a few inches. Standing in nothing but his boxers, he looked at me through the crack with sleepy eyes.

"What's shakin' motherfucker?"

"Jesus H. Christ, Peeb. Any reason you gave an order that no one could tell me what the fuck's goin' on?"

I shrugged. "Wanted to show you myself, so I told the fellas to keep it quiet. You gonna let me in?"

"It's five o'clock in the morning, be fuckin' quiet," he whispered. "She's still sleeping."

"She's here?"

"Yeah, she's here," he said. "Now shut the fuck up and come in."

"Nice seeing you, too."

I walked past him and toward his kitchen. I needed a beer, and I needed one bad. As soon as I stepped into the dining room, I grinned.

On the center of the table, a glass sat. Filled with what looked like pink water, it was a reminder of what a good solid bitch Peyton Price was.

I motioned toward the glass. "She make that for me?"

He nodded. "We went to the hospital and got her checked out. They did some tests for diseases and some other shit. She claimed she got drunk and agreed to let a bunch of guys fuck her. Doctors didn't believe her at first, but she convinced 'em in no time. Tell you what, that's one strong fuckin' woman. Anyway, when we got back, she made that for you. Been sittin' there since about 10:00. She fell asleep at 2:00. She's been worried about ya. She's not the only one."

I wagged my eyebrows at him. "Alive and well, motherfucker."

"Tell me what happened."

"I'm getting' to it." I pulled off my backpack, unzipped it, and removed the four Zip-Lock bags.

He glanced at the bags. His face distorted, and then he looked at me. "What the fuck is *that*?"

I tossed the bags on the table. "Cocks. Four of 'em."

"You cut off their fuckin' dicks?"

"Sliced off their cocks and their balls. All four of 'em," I said. "Well, four cocks, and eight nuts. Cut the fuckers off right at the base, too. Didn't even leave 'em a stub. Was Cholo's idea. Said that's how they do it in Mexico. Figured if it was good enough for the cartel, it was good enough for me."

I picked up the glass of pink liquid and downed it in one drink. "You have one of these yet?"

"Seriously?" he snapped back.

His mouth curled into a smirk.

"You did, didn't ya?"

He nodded. "Don't tell anybody. Fucking shit was pretty good."

"Man, I'm tellin' ya. It's good as fuck."

"Is that you, Pee Bee?"

"Hey, Peyton," I said. "How you feelin'?"

"Just tired," she said. "Other than that, I'm fine."

She walked into the dining room in one of Crip's poker runs shirts from 2011 and a pair of his boxers.

Crip reached for the sacks of cocks, but it was too late. She'd already seen them.

"What are *those*?" she asked.

"Just…" Crip swung his hand across the table and tried to scoop up the sacks, but knocked one of them onto the floor in front of her.

She bent down and picked it up. She lifted the blood-filled sack and stared at it. "Gross. What is it?"

Crip shrugged and glanced at me. Then, she looked at me. Pretty soon, Crip followed.

Thanks, motherfucker.

I cleared my throat. "One of those fella's cocks."

She wrinkled her nose. "Seriously?"

"Yep."

"You cut off their cocks?"

"Yep."

"Like, off?"

I pointed at the bag. "Off enough that it's in that Zip-Lock bag, yeah."

"The whole thing?"

"Cut em off at the base," I said. "Their nuts, too."

She looked at Crip. The other three sacks of cocks were clutched in his right hand. He shrugged, and eventually started laughing.

"It ain't funny," I said. "You ever cut off a man's cock? Kinda gross, if you ask me. Bleeds a lot, too."

"What are we going to do with them?" Peyton asked.

"We?" I asked. "We? I'm done with 'em"

"Can I flush 'em?"

Crip eyes widened. "You want to flush 'em?"

Peyton grinned. "I do."

He shrugged. "They're about the side of a good turd. I suppose they'd flush."

She stood up and reached for the other three bags. "I want to."

I reached into my pocket, and pulled out a pair of rubber gloves. All along, I figured I'd be in charge of the disposal. "Here," I said. "You'll need these."

She took the gloves. "Thanks. Be back in a minute."

Crip and I looked at each other, but we didn't talk while she was gone. After the toilet flushed six or eight times, the sound of running water followed. Then, she walked past us and into the kitchen.

"Trash bags?"

"Under the sink," Crip said.

"Here." She handed me neatly folded a trash sack. "You probably want to throw that away somewhere else. Or burn it. Get rid of the DNA."

I looked at Crip. He shrugged.

"I needed that," Peyton said. "You know; victims of sexual abuse say they need closure. Well, flushing their dicks down the toilet felt pretty fucking good."

I made a fist and held it at the center of the table. "Good enough?"

She pounded her fist into mine. "Good enough."

And, just like that, those two words made riding around all night with a bunch of cocks in Zip-Lock bags worth it.

NINETEEN

NICK

I pulled into the driveway, turned the bike to face the street, and shut off the ignition. After a deep breath, I stepped over the gas tank and brushed the wrinkles from my jeans. The short walk up the driveway brought back memories, but it always did.

And it always would.

I knocked three times on the door.

"Enter!"

I pushed the door open. My father was sitting in *his* chair watching the news. He still resembled the military man he spent his lifetime being, his buzz-cut hair and athletic physique were a testament to his devotion to the Navy. Retired after 30 years in the military, he was now employed as a groundskeeper at a golf course. In his mind, however, he was simply on extended leave from the Navy.

"Get another tattoo?" he asked.

Nice to see you, too.

"Who is it?" my mother asked, her voice coming from the kitchen.

"It's Nick, and he's got a new tattoo," my father shouted. "A god damned bumblebee. On his neck."

"Let him in for heaven's sake."

"He's already in. Wouldn't be seeing his tattoo if he was still on the porch."

"The tattoo's old, Pop. Been there for a few years."

"It's dark." He got out of his chair and glared. "Looks new."

"It's not."

He studied my neck for a moment, then glanced over the patches on my kutte. "So, who died?"

"Nobody died, Pop. Just came to talk to mom."

"Elizabeth, he's here to see *you*."

I shook my head and walked past him. "I'm here to see *both of you*."

"Well, when you and your bumblebee get done talking to your mother, I'll be here."

To the unknowing bystander, my father would appear to be an asshole. Truthfully, he wasn't. He had an opinion about everything, and offered it whether the recipient liked it or not, but he meant no harm in doing so. Over the years, I learned to dismiss a good part of what he said as being nothing more than bullshit.

"We'll both come back and see ya," I said in a sarcastic tone.

I stepped into the kitchen. My mother stood at the sink washing dishes.

"Why don't you use the dishwasher?"

"It doesn't get them clean."

"It's got a heat exchanger that superheats the water. It's gets them clean *and* sterilizes them."

"This is relaxing," she said.

She turned her head to the side and waited. I pressed my lips to her cheek and kissed her. "How's work?"

"Long hours. One of these days, I'll retire, but I don't know when. I'll be done in just a minute."

HARD

"No hurry," I said.

I opened the fridge, rummaged through each of the Tupperware containers, and eventually found some fried chicken. I grabbed a few pieces and sat down at the dining room table.

"Get a plate."

"I don't need a plate. It'd just be one more to wash."

"Get something to drink so you don't choke. That chicken was dry. I don't know what happened to it."

"I'm fine. And the chicken's good. Really."

At the same time that I finished the second piece of chicken, she got done with the dishes. After drying her hands and tossing the towel on the countertop, she sat down at my side.

"You never come over just to see us, so what's going on, Nicholas?"

I tossed the chicken bones in the trash, washed my hands, and sat down. "I've got some questions about a girl."

Her eyes lit up. "Did you meet a girl?"

"Settle down. I met a girl, but it's not what you think. There's nothing going on."

She smiled. "Why are you asking about her?"

I shrugged. "I just want to make sure she's going to be okay. Something happened to her."

She placed her hand on my forearm. "Is she okay?"

"I don't know. She seems to be."

My mother worked as a counselor for a sexual assault center, and had for as long as I could remember. Her lifetime of exposure to domestic violence, sexual abuse, and other traumatic events women experienced made her a wealth of information on the subjects.

She gripped my forearm. "What's bothering you?"

"Don't go gettin' all mad, just listen, okay?"

"Okay."

I stared at the center of the table, and tried to speak without emotion, but it wasn't easy. "If a girl is gang raped by four men, is it possible that she will recover from it without counseling?"

"Oh, Nicholas," her hand shot up and covered her mouth. "I'm so sorry."

I shifted my eyes to meet hers. She looked overwhelmed.

"Recover? No. Not without professional help. Survive? Sure. She can survive, but her choice to not seek counseling is foolish. The center should be able to get her all the help she needs. Have her call me."

"She doesn't want counseling."

"Why isn't she following the recommendations of her case worker?"

"It's complicated. She didn't report it as a rape. She doesn't want to."

She shook her head. "She still can. And she needs to. It's part of the process that she needs to go through. Tell her to report it."

"She won't. She's stubborn."

She sighed. "The men who did this need to be brought to justice."

My eyes fell to the table. While I contemplated what to say next, she squeezed my arm.

"Nicholas..."

I met her gaze, but didn't respond.

"Nicholas..."

She gripped my arm firmly. "Nicholas Michael Navarro. I'm your mother. Remember, you came from my womb. I know you all too well. What did you do?"

I shrugged. "They've been brought to justice, Mom. Believe me."

"What did you do?"

Lying to my mother wasn't possible. Providing very little detail was my only option. "Just trust me. They've been dealt with."

She sighed. "Your friend needs help. What's her name? I'll pray for her."

"Her name doesn't matter."

"Tell me her name so I can include her in my prayers."

I needed all the help I could get. "Peyton."

She nodded and released my arm. "You've got a convincing way about you, Nicholas. Convince your friend to get help. If nothing else, bring her in to see me."

I stood up. "I'm not bringing her in."

"People listen to you. They always have. God gave you a gift. Use it." She reached out and poked me in the chest. "And what did I tell you about wearing that thing in this house?"

"I was in a hurry."

"I wish you'd grow up and get out of that gang. I feel like we failed you every time I see you wearing that thing."

"It's not a gang, it's a club."

"Call it whatever makes you feel better about it. It's a gang. And, when you wear it, you're a gang member. You're going to get shot one of these days, and probably for nothing more than wearing that ridiculous thing. Get your friend some help. And go talk to your father, he misses you."

"Thanks, Mom. I love you."

She hugged me and kissed my cheek. "I love you, too."

She told me exactly what I expected. Peyton's hope of sweeping her assault under the rug wasn't going to work. If she wanted to recover, she would need to seek the help of a professional.

I walked into the living room.

My father cleared his throat. "Sit down."

I sat on the sofa across from him. He reached for the remote control, turned up the volume on the television, and leaned forward in his seat.

"They still alive?"

I wrinkled my brow. "Who?"

He arched his brow.

My father may have been elderly by most people's standards, but his hearing was fantastic. His service in the Navy taught him to be attentive, if nothing else.

I glanced over my shoulder. My mother was putting up the dishes. I turned to face him. "For now."

He relaxed in his seat, folded his arms across his chest, and exhaled. "Don't you dare get caught."

"I wasn't involved, Pop. I'm clean on this one."

He shook his head. "You and I? We're a lot alike. I raised you, remember? It isn't over. If it was, you wouldn't be here. Remember your training, don't be driven by anger, and don't get caught."

I nodded. "Thanks."

"Fucking judge gave some kid six months for raping a girl the other day. You see that shit on the news? She was incoherent and drunk, and the little prick raped her."

I nodded. The case disgusted me. "Yes, Sir. I sure did."

"When a man rapes a woman, he doesn't just rape *her*. He rapes her entire life. She's forced to live a life with the pain from that memory for a lifetime. And for that judge to send a message that six months in county jail is a fair trade for what happened to that woman?" He sat up in his chair, clenched his jaw, and took a long breath through his nose. "I'd like to get my hands on that judge and that kid."

"You and me both, Pop."

"I can forgive a lot of things. Rape isn't one of 'em."

I didn't want to talk about it any longer. The more I thought about it, the angrier I was becoming. I stood up. "Yeah? Me neither."

He could tell my blood was boiling. After studying me for a moment, he lowered his chin slightly. "Love you, Son."

"Love you, too."

TWENTY

PEYTON

Although it seemed my mind was elsewhere, I sat at my desk and attempted to manufacture a story out of minimal facts and zero desire.

"Working your magic?"

The sound of Mr. Rollins' voice made me cringe. I had no story, no passion to write one, and for the first time that I was aware of, didn't really care about performing my job or exposing the facts.

"It's coming pretty slow," I responded.

"It'll come. It always does. At least for you."

I grinned and turned toward the monitor. "I hope so."

"Anything I can do to help?"

"Just give me some time."

"Take all the time you need," he said. "Just make sure you get it right in the end."

"Okay, thanks."

"Let me know if you need anything."

I nodded. "Will do."

I stared at the screen while my hands hovered over the keyboard. After several minutes of zero productivity, I opened my browser, did a search for any information about the Savages being hospitalized, and found nothing.

Disappointed, I closed the browser, and began to type.

The life of an outlaw biker is one that most individuals will never completely comprehend. I have had the luxury of being exposed to one such group, the Filthy F*ckers MC, for some time.

In doing so, I have learned

I stopped typing, read what I had written, and erased everything. Frustrated, I picked up my phone and sent Navarro a text message, hopeful that he'd respond favorably. It was a long shot, but well worth a try.

Want to grab lunch? No interview. Just lunch??

I tossed the phone on my desk, looked around my office, and decided it was a disastrous mess. Thirty seconds into the reorganization of my entire library, my phone beeped.

I picked it up, hopeful, but without much expectation.

Please say yes. Please say yes. Please say yes.

The message was from Navarro.

Meet me at the clubhouse in 30?

I smiled, typed *yes* as my response, and paused. After erasing the one-word message, I re-typed my response.

Thank you.

TWENTY-ONE

NICK

Standing in the clubhouse parking lot, I stared at my bike and tried to imagine it with paint on it. "I don't think the fucker will look any *better*. It'll just look different."

Pee Bee cocked his head to the side and studied the rusty gas tank. "Up to you. Been lookin' like shit as long as I've known ya. Don't know why you're wantin' to paint it now."

I shrugged. "Just thinking about making a change."

"Changin' your bike ain't gonna change anything, Crip. When you get done, your life's still gonna be here."

"Well holy fucking shit. Listen to you. What? You a certified fucking therapist now?"

"No."

"So why you trying to tell me how to live my life?"

"I'm not."

I lifted my leg over the seat, sat down, and draped my arms over the handlebars. "Sure sounds like it."

"I don't like it, either, motherfucker. Not even a little bit. But I can't fuckin' change it. Only thing we can do is keep on keepin' on. That's it."

"Thanks for the words of wisdom, Peeb."

"Whatever I can do to help, asshole."

HARD

I gazed toward the street, not really focusing on anything. The building we used for a clubhouse was in Oceanside, twenty miles north of San Diego. The city was the home for many Marines stationed in Camp Pendleton, which was a few miles north. Along with the neighboring cities of Carlsbad and Vista, the overall population was about 200,000.

Our location was on a street that had minimal traffic, making passing cars something of an oddity. The unmarked police car that was approaching stood out like a dick on a wedding cake.

"Fucking hell."

Pee Bee's eyes widened. "What?"

"My three o'clock. Cop."

"No shit?"

He turned toward the street. "Looks like your fuckin' buddy."

He was right. The car and the driver looked pretty god damned familiar. It was none other than detective shit-for-brains, the man who arrested me in the shop.

"Here he comes," I said.

He pulled in the lot, rolled up alongside us, and came to a stop.

He rolled down the window and poked his head out. "You know, on some days, I wish I didn't have to work," he said. "I could just hang around, sit on my motorcycle and look mean. Wouldn't that be the life?"

"Only a couple of problems with that, *detective*."

He lowered his sunglasses and peered over the top of the frames. "You know I've got to ask. The problems? What are they, Navarro?"

I stepped off my bike, folded my arms in front of my chest, and flexed my biceps. "You don't have a *motorcycle*, and you look like a *pussy*."

He laughed a sarcastic laugh, opened the car door, and stepped out.

He removed his mirrored cop glasses and hung them on the collar of his police-issue polo shirt. "That's funny."

"I'm the club joker. Jokes? I got a million of 'em. Something I can help you with, *detective*?"

"Maybe. And, just so you know, I'm not on a fact finding mission. I'm really just here to make you…" He glanced at Pee Bee. "…and your cohort aware of something."

"So you stopped by to talk to Peeb and me?"

"That his name?" he nodded toward Pee Bee. "Peeb?"

"No. Name's Pee Bee, but I call him Peeb."

"Pee Bee, huh? What's that stand for?"

"Peanut Butter," Pee Bee said. "One of the other fellas is named Jelly. We're fuckin' besties."

He alternated glances between Pee Bee and me. "You two should come on down to La Jolla and get a job at *The Comedy Store*. Shit, you could get rich, funny as you two pricks are."

I cleared my throat. "Never much cared for the smell of pork, *detective*. And we're getting' ready to ride out of here. What can I do for you?"

"This entire state is filled with outlaw motorcycle clubs. Personally, I never gave a shit one way or another about most of 'em. You know, you guys kind of clean up your own messes. Makes it nice for people in my line of work."

"Get to your point," I said.

"Well, there's one local club I always kind of detested. Maybe you've heard of 'em. Satan's Savages. Bunch of shit birds, if you ask me. Always flexing their muscle, and trying to be something they're not. They want to be like the big boys. You know, the Mongols or Hells

HARD

Angels..." He shook his head. "But they can't."

With my arms still crossed in front of my chest, I stared back at him. "What's this have to do with us?"

"I'm getting to that. So, a few nights back, we got several reports of a group of bikers riding through town. A big group. Maybe sixty or so. It was late at night, which isn't when most outlaw MCs are out and about in full force, unless something's going down. With no reports of violence or gunfire, we really had no reason to react, because riding motorcycles in itself isn't a crime. So we waited. Then, late that night, one of Satan's Savages showed up at Scripps Mercy. Someone had cut his cock clean off. Castrated him too. Thirty minutes after that, two more showed up at Kindred. Same damned thing. Relieved of their cocks and balls."

I cocked an eyebrow. "Wasn't some kind of club initiation, was it? Cut off your cock to jump from prospect to patch?"

Pee Bee laughed out loud, but the detective remained straight-faced.

"All three of 'em claimed it was an ISIS attack. They said some towel-heads did it." he paused and forced a laugh. "So, about five in the morning, the president of Satan's Savages shows up at Scripps. His cock had been cut off so short he was left with a twat. But one thing that was different about him was that he'd been shot. Once in each leg with a .45 caliber."

"Same thing? Towel-heads?" I asked.

"No," he replied. "Said he cut himself shaving. When we asked him about the gunshot wounds, he said he didn't even notice 'em. Crazy prick rode his motorcycle to the hospital. He'd lost so much blood they had to give him a transfusion."

"But all four of 'em lived?"

The detective nodded. "It's a damned shame, but they did. Which is why I'm here."

"Why *are* you here?" I asked.

"Never cared for the president of that group. The Savages," he said. "Had him on a couple of rape cases a few years back, but neither of them materialized. Sad thing about rapists is that they seem to maintain a pattern of repeating the crimes. Considering the facts of this case, and that someone cut his cock off, my guess is that he dipped his dick in the wrong skank."

I clenched my jaw at the thought of him calling Peyton a skank. "So you came by to tell us this, why?"

"Like I said in the beginning. I don't mind MC's. They have their own means of administering justice, which saves me time, and saves the taxpayers money. Rumor has it that Whipple and his boys are going after whoever did this. You might get the word out."

"So, you want Peeb and me to spread the word that four dickless bikers are looking for revenge?"

He put his glasses on, pressed them high on his nose and got in his car. He then draped his right arm out the car window, brushed his left palm up his arm, and lifted the sleeve of his polo shirt slightly. "No, I want you to finish what you started."

My eyes locked on the tattoo in the center of his bicep.

An eagle, trident, anchor, and pistol.

"Have a nice day," he said.

And he drove away.

"That was fuckin' weird," Pee Bee said.

"Sure was."

I waited to see if Peeb was going to mention the tattoo, but it never came.

HARD

After a few minutes of small talk and trying to decide if we were going to stay at the shop and drink beer or go eat lunch, my phone beeped.

Anxious to see if it was Peyton, I pulled it from my pocket and read the message.

"Peyton wants to go to lunch. You want to go?"

He shrugged. "Long as you don't mind, sure."

"I don't mind. And she might like the company."

"Sounds good. It's almost noon now, want to meet her somewhere?"

"I'll just have her meet us here." I said as I typed her a text message. "I'll see if she wants to ride. Maybe it'll will clear her mind."

And maybe it'll clear mine, too.

TWENTY-TWO

PEYTON

I sat on the hard fender with my hands at his waist and tilted my head back. Riding on the back of Navarro's bike was like flying, and each time I did it, I grew a little fonder of it. While we rode along Mission Beach Boulevard looking for a place to eat, I thought of the phrase *as free as a bird*, and wondered if most bikers felt no differently than I did.

Riding was an unexplainable thrill, something that words couldn't come close to accurately describing, but the word *flying* immediately came to mind. With the feeling of flight came a sense of freedom.

When I recognized the sense of freedom, it all made sense.

The outlaw biker really wanted nothing more than to be left to his own devices. The ride freed them from the clutch of whatever it was that brought them to drop their respective asses into the seat in the first place.

The satisfaction from riding seemed to be much different after the incident. Before, I enjoyed it immensely, but other than the thrill of being on the back of the bike, nothing else *happened*. After the incident, the ride seemed to rid me of all contamination, leaving me feeling cleansed of everything that was impure.

I couldn't help but wonder if each and every hard-core biker had some underlying reason – some catastrophe in their life – that made

HARD

riding more of a necessity, and not merely a simple desire.

We parked in front of a small taco shop. I adjusted my hair tie and reluctantly released Navarro's waist. "I have a lot of questions to ask while we're waiting on food."

He stepped off the bike and steadied it for me to get off. "I thought you'd be done with that article by now."

"Actually, I haven't even started," I said. "But this has nothing to do with the article. Not really."

"Ask me anything you want," Pee Bee said. "But prepare for the truth. I won't bullshit you like Ol' Crip."

I climbed off the fender. "How did he get his name?"

Navarro shot me a look. I winked at him.

"Crip. Short for cripple. Because he's an old man."

I looked at Navarro. "True?"

He nodded. "That's what it stands for, but I'm far from an old man."

"What about yours," I asked Pee Bee.

"P. B.," Navarro said. "Pretty Boy. Because he looks like a bearded girl."

I laughed. "Pretty Boy and Crip. I like it."

"Come on," Pee Bee said. "I've got to feed the machine."

I followed them into the restaurant, feeling much better than when I was at work. Riding was therapeutic, and whether or not I wanted to admit it, I needed a little therapy in my life.

"Why do you ride?" I asked Navarro as we sat down.

"Me?"

I nodded. "Yes, you."

"Big picture?"

"Sure."

He folded his fingers together as if he was preparing to pray. I studied his tattooed knuckles. On his upper knuckles, the word *STAY*. On the lower, *REAL*. It was easy to get lost in admiring his tattoos, and I enjoyed doing it.

"It's hard to explain," he said. "I get a sense of freedom when I ride that I can't seem to get anywhere else. Being in a cage makes me feel like I'm locked up. Like an animal. The difference between riding and driving is the difference between a tiger in the wild, and one in a zoo."

"And by *cage*, you mean a car?"

"Yep. A car is a cage. That's what we call 'em, anyway. Write that in your little fucking article."

"I like that. And, I reserve the right to use it." I turned to Pee Bee. "What about you?"

"You like rollercoasters?"

I grinned. "Love 'em."

He arched a brow. "Love 'em, or like 'em a lot?"

"Love 'em."

"Can you imagine riding one to work? And home? Like every day? Wouldn't that be fuckin' cool?"

"I wish there was one that went from my townhouse to my office. That'd be awesome."

"I ride for the same reason people ride a roller coaster or jump off a cliff. It thrills me. Basically, I've got a rollercoaster that takes me everywhere."

"Drinks?" the waitress asked.

"Budweiser."

"Budweiser."

"And you?" she asked.

HARD

"Budweiser," I responded.

"Menus are on in the condiment caddy, I'll be back in a few."

"What's good here?"

"Fish tacos," Pee Bee said. "Don't even look at the menu, just order."

"Seriously?"

"Bitch, do I look like I'd steer you wrong?"

He wasn't as tattooed as Navarro. Hell, no one was. But both of his upper biceps had tattoos, each of his shoulders were covered in a tribal pattern, and he had a star tattooed on his upper forearms.

To the unknowing, he looked like a thug.

But I knew deep down inside that he'd never steer me wrong.

"No," I said.

He raked his fingers through his long hair and leaned back in his seat. "Then get the fish tacos."

The waitress brought our drinks. "Three Bud's."

She handed us the bottles of beer. "Had a chance to look at the menu?"

"Don't need to," I said. "I want the fish tacos."

"One order of fish tacos."

She looked at Pee Bee. "And you?"

"Fish tacos."

"What about you?"

Navarro's mouth curled into a smirk. "Give me the pork chili verde. Corn tortillas."

"Just couldn't go for the fish tacos?" She joked. "Make it easy?"

"I'm a non-conformist, and nothing's ever easy for me," he responded.

"What a surprise," she said.

I didn't totally agree, but I kept my mouth shut. In my opinion, Navarro was a non-conformist, but I believed life was extremely easy for him.

All Navarro had to do to succeed in life was be Navarro.

And being Navarro, at least for him, came naturally.

TWENTY-THREE

NICK

My opinion was all that mattered. If someone didn't share my views, they were wrong, because I was always right. Being exposed to life-changing events seemed to be the only thing to ever get me to look at life – or myself – with honest eyes.

Pee Bee and I stood in the shop, solving the world's problems, one at a time. The conversation soon included talk of Peyton, and to my surprise, he didn't accept it well.

"How the fuck am I supposed to answer that? I'm not you, and you sure as fuck aren't me. It really don't matter what I say, you're gonna come back with some bullshit and tell me I'm either dumb or crazy. When we're done talkin', you'll be right. Because you're always fuckin' right," Pee Bee said.

I kicked a small stone across the floor of the shop, then met his gaze. "I asked you. I want your opinion."

"I think you're reacting to what Whip and them did. You know, in Pete's bar."

I shook my head. "I think it's more than that."

He shrugged. "Like I said. I give an opinion. You shoot it down."

"I didn't *shoot it down*."

He picked at his fingernails for a few long seconds, then cleared his

HARD

throat. "All I know is this. Been knowin' you for damned near ten years. You ain't never had – and you ain't never wanted – an Ol' Lady--"

"I didn't say I wanted--"

He leaned forward and shot me a glare. "Motherfucker, let me finish."

I took a drink of my beer and nodded. "Fine. Finish."

"Where was I?" His eyes fell to the floor. He rubbed his beard for a minute, then looked up. "Oh, yeah. So, you always say how you don't need an Ol' Lady. Fellas with Ol' Ladies aren't devoted to the club. When Stretch had that Ol' Lady from El Cajon, you told me his devotion to the club went to shit, and he needed to get rid of her. Remember that?"

I nodded. "I do, but--"

He raised his hand in the air. "Motherfucker, I ain't done."

I sighed. "Continue."

"Okay. So you don't like Ol' Ladies, and you bang bitches like the rest of us. Hit 'em and quit 'em. Some cute little bitch with an attitude comes along, and you start beatin' that little pussy of hers up. Well, here's my point." He crossed his arms and shot me a glare. "All you was doin' was fuckin' her. That's it. Never would have amounted to shit. When she was done with that article, I *guarantee* you that you'd have kicked her to the side."

"What's your fucking point, Peeb?" I tossed my empty bottle toward the trash can, missed, and it crashed to the floor and shattered.

He nodded his head toward the trash can. "See what I mean? There you go, tryin' to intimidate me."

"What?"

"Bustin' bottles and shit. Subliminal stuff. You ain't tryin' to hear what I got to say."

I shook my head and turned toward the fridge. "I missed the trash can. And your little speech made no sense."

"I was tryin' to be nice."

"Since when are you nice?"

"Fine, motherfucker. How about *this*," he snapped back. "Until Whip and them fellas raped her, you didn't give a fuck about her or how she felt. All you cared about was dippin' your dick. Then, they raped her. All of a sudden, you feel like you gotta take care of her."

I opened my beer and stared back at him. "Not true."

"True as fuck."

I shook my head. "She's been different since she came to the shop on the first day."

"Grab me a beer, motherfucker." He motioned toward the fridge. "Different how?"

I shrugged. "She surfs, snowboards, fucking bungie jumps, drives a Jeep--"

"She drives a Jeep? She drives a fucking Jeep?" He burst into laughter, and eventually caught his breath. "That's your excuse?"

"Amongst other things."

"There's 200,000 bitches in SD that drive Jeeps."

"Like you said earlier, asshole. I wasn't done."

"Hurry the fuck up and *get* done," he said. "I got another point to make."

I turned to the fridge, grabbed another beer, and handed it to him. "All the things she does aren't important. The fact she does them is."

"What the fuck does that mean?"

"It defines what type of person she is. She's adventurous."

"And that's what you like about her?"

HARD

I nodded. "Yep."

"That's what you're lookin' for in life?"

"I'm not looking to get fucking married, Peeb. Not even to have an Ol' Lady. I was just saying that I enjoy it when she's around, and I hoped she keeps coming around after the article's done."

"And you say you're sayin' all this because she's adventurous?"

I nodded. "Yep."

He glared at me while he took a long drink of beer.

He lowered the bottle and wiped his beard with his free hand. "Why didn't you put an ad on Craigslist five years ago? *Tattooed biker seeks adventurous bitch. Must drive Jeep and bungie jump.*"

"Now you're being an asshole."

He chuckled. "Don't get me wrong, I like the little bitch. She seems to be a solid motherfucker. I mean, if you're askin' me. But you sayin' you're wantin' to keep her around and shit just makes me think it's for the wrong fuckin' reasons."

"What if I was saying it, and she hadn't been raped?"

"But she was."

"I'm asking you, asshole. What if she wasn't?"

He shrugged. "It'd be a different story. I'd probably say somethin' like, *damn, Crip, you're finally settlin' down.*"

"I'm not settling down. I'm saying I enjoy her company."

He finished his beer, tossed the empty bottle into the trash can, and met my gaze. "I guess all I'm sayin' is this. Don't enjoy it for the wrong reasons."

Standing there staring back at him, I had no response to give. All I could do was hope that what I felt was a result of a clear mind, not a sympathetic one.

TWENTY-FOUR

PEYTON

The weather in the San Diego's area was perfect, at least in my opinion. Spring and early summer temperatures were in the high 60's and low 70's. Navarro and I sat at the coffee shop, enveloped in silence. As the early-morning sun warmed my legs, I wondered just why he had scheduled our morning meeting.

He rocked his chair on its rear legs. "Got anything for me to read yet?"

"The article?"

"Yeah."

It seemed things between us had become awkward. At least much more than before. It had been two weeks since the incident, and although I felt much better about everything, I certainly didn't feel *normal*. I wondered if he sensed it, or if he had reasons of his own for being someone other than his natural self.

"No," I said. "Not yet."

He dropped the chair back down on its legs and reached for his coffee. "What's the hold up?"

"Hold up?" I shot him an evil stare. The real kind, not the friendly version. "Have you ever written anything for publication?"

He looked at me like I had three heads. "No."

"Well," I said. "It isn't easy. I'm trying to decide where to take it. And we're not done with the interviews."

"I was just asking."

I was tired of people asking. Camden asked every time he saw me. Navarro was asking. I even asked myself, but lately those times had become infrequent.

"It'll be done when it's done. And, when I'm done with it, you'll be the first to know. You've got to proof it, remember?"

He took a drink of coffee and nodded. "Just asking."

I took a sip of my latte and studied him. Relaxed in his seat with his coffee in his hand, his shoulders were rolled forward. His broad chest looked deflated, and he seemed considerably smaller than he actually was.

"What's been wrong with you lately?" I asked, the words coming out before I had a chance to stop them.

I wanted him to be the way he was when I met him. Rough. Aggressive. Angry. In-you-face.

But something was different.

He rocked the chair on its back legs again. "What do you mean?"

"Look at you." I shrugged. "You're docile."

He shot me a look, but it was forced, and I couldn't really identify it. "Docile?"

I nodded. "Compliant. Unassertive. Accommodating. You know, docile."

"No I'm not."

"Okay. Whatever. Let's go get some ice cream."

"Now?"

"Yeah. Right now. I want ice cream."

He stood up. "You gonna bring your coffee with you?"

"See? That's what I'm talking about. A month ago you would have told me to fuck off, and you would have shoved your cock down my throat to shut me up. Now? Now you're different."

He loomed over me with a blank look on his face.

"Sit down," I said.

He complied, sitting back in his seat. He looked defeated. I wondered if I was being shallow and insensitive. I quickly decided maybe I was simply being selfish, and that something may have happened in his life that I was unaware of.

"I'm sorry. It's just. Here lately, you're different. Like I said, you've been kind of soft and passive. Is there anything you want to talk about?"

He shook his head. "No. How about you?"

"Me? I'm not different. I'm the same. You? You're--" I paused and waved my hand toward him. "You're not *you*."

He took a drink of his coffee and leaned forward. "Can I speak freely?"

"Sure."

"I'm worried about you."

I wrinkled my nose. "Me?"

He nodded. "Yeah, you."

"Why?"

"You came to me and were some cute bitch that was going to write an article about my club. I was flattered, excited, and pretty gung-ho about the whole deal. Add to it that you're cute as fuck, and it made everything that much better. Or worse. Or whatever. So, I invite you to the clubhouse." He leaned back in his chair, rubbed his beard, then sighed heavily. "You asked questions and I answered. It was interesting, and I actually enjoyed it. Then. We fucked. Enjoyed that, too."

So did I.

He paused and shook his head. "Then, one day we got coffee and we went to get lunch. That day we went to lunch? I was having a pretty good time with you on the back of the bike. Actually wondered for a minute what it'd be like having you around. Never met a tough little bitch like you. Thought you were pretty fucking good stuff."

I wasn't sure where he was going with the conversation, but hearing him say how he felt warmed me much more than the morning sun. I never would have guessed being called a bitch could be such a rewarding experience, but it was.

His face went solemn, but didn't last long. An angry look soon replaced it. "Then, they raped you. And, I'm worried. I want you to be the same, but I wonder if you ever will be. I wish it never would have happened."

I started to speak, but the words got caught in my throat. I sat and stared, incapable of speaking and not really sure what feelings – if any – my face was conveying.

I was filled with anger. I didn't want what took place to have happened either, but it did. Afterward, all I wanted was for things in my life – and for me – to be the same, but I knew they never would be. The fact that four complete strangers viciously stole my chance of having a perfect life from me and left me feeling guilty, filthy, and forever tainted caused me to feel pain that I never knew existed.

"I feel responsible," he said.

My response was dry and coarse. "Don't."

"I can't help it."

"You know," I said.

My eyes began to well with tears. I fought not to cry, but wondered how long it would last. "That day? I keep replaying the morning in my head. When I decided to go get the recorder. I should have called the bar. I knew the name of it. I could have. But I didn't. I wanted to go in there *without* calling. I wanted to put on my big girl panties and go to the biker bar without you. Sit where we sat. Do some research. Watch who…watch who came and went. If I would have called, and maybe gone ten minutes…ten minutes…"

He raised his hand, trying to get me to stop.

But I needed to finish.

He stood.

I waved him off, and then realized tears were dripping off my chin and onto my lap.

I cleared my throat. "Ten minutes. Just ten minutes later. Ten fucking minutes."

I wiped my face with the tips of my fingers. "So, somehow… somehow I convinced myself it's all my fault."

His jaw was tight, and he was breathing through his nose. He was angry, but I knew he wasn't angry with me. He shook his head. "It's not your fault."

I bit down on my lower lip and tried to stop it from quivering. It did very little to calm me. I was taught not to hate, but I hated the men that did what they did to me. Cutting their cocks off might have satisfied everyone else, but it didn't satisfy me, no matter what I tried to tell myself.

"Can you just…could you…hold…"

I wanted him to hold me, but I couldn't say it.

The crying got worse, almost turning into a full-blown blubber.

HARD

Everything just seemed to come crashing down, and I began to feel heavy inside. My heart began to ache. I closed my eyes and wondered what I had ever done to deserve feeling the way I felt.

Nothing.

Life wasn't fair.

I closed my eyes and cried, wishing Navarro wasn't watching. I wanted to be in North Carolina, where my father could comfort me. As I wept, and wished things were different, I felt Navarro's arms around my waist.

He lifted me from my seat and held me in my arms.

But the pain never stopped.

TWENTY-FIVE

NICK

While at war, I initially struggled with taking another man's life. When the time came to act, doing so didn't come as a decision I made, it was more of a reaction. An instinct to survive. Contrary to the belief of many, Soldiers, Sailors, and Marines during wartime didn't kill without cause. In almost every circumstance when I was required to take a life, doing so was to protect myself or my fellow SEALs from being killed.

At no point did the value of another man's life diminish, but the decision to kill became much less of a struggle. In the end I decided I had become insensitive and damaged.

A byproduct of war.

My decision to start the MC was done to rid my mind of the day-to-day demons that seemed to take possession of my soul after the war ended. It worked, but I was left void of the voices in my head that somehow provided justification for the atrocities of war. What remained was a soulless shell with the body and mind of an insensitive killer.

I pointed the barrel of the pistol at his head and sighed. "I struggled with this, you know. I told myself it wasn't necessary, but it is."

The muscles in his jaw went tight. "Do what you gotta do."

It was the first time I'd seen him since our fight in the bar. No differently than Peyton, I regretted decisions that I had made, and wondered if I should have just killed him and Panda the day they came into our bar.

I could have even done something when they trespassed on our turf.

Had I acted on either of those occasions, Peyton's life would have been as it was before. Filled with guilt, sorrow, and a tremendous amount of hatred, I stared back at him. In his eyes, I saw nothing. No regret, no sorrow, not even fear. I wanted to say so much. I had envisioned giving a long speech, telling him how murdering him was the final step in serving justice for the life he had chosen to live. For the pain that he caused so many others.

Instead, I simply pointed the pistol at his forehead and pulled the trigger.

He fell to the floor with a heavy thud. The carpet around him slowly darkened as the blood poured out of the cavity in his skull.

I felt no differently. I expected to be cured. Free of pain. To immediately believe that Peyton's life would quickly transform back to normal.

But I wasn't cured.

My heart still ached.

Filled with the belief that the only cure for what I was feeling would be the passage of time, I stepped over Whip's body and walked away.

TWENTY-SIX

PEYTON

I pushed the door open and met the receptionist's gaze. After scanning the lobby and finding it empty, I proceeded to walk toward her. With each step, my legs felt heavier, a little less capable.

Eventually, I made it to her work station. She looked up at me and smiled. I smiled in return.

"Hi. I uhhm. I need to talk to someone."

"Are you looking for anyone in particular?"

"Uhhm. I mean. No. Well, kind of. Someone who. Someone who has. I'd really like it if. Do you have any women?"

She looked caring. Understanding. And confused.

"Are you a victim?"

My lip began to quiver. I clutched my purse and nodded. "Uh huh."

She lifted her hand and reached toward me. "I'll get you one of our counselors, and if needed, an EMDR therapist."

I took her hand in mine. I wanted to tell her *thank you*, but lately it seemed wanting to speak and actually speaking were two totally different things.

Either her hand was shaking or mine was, but together, we stood there and shook like it was the right thing to do.

"What's your name, beautiful?" she asked.

HARD

"I'm Peyton," I said. "Peyton Price."

"I'm Candace," she said. "I'm a survivor. It's going to get better, okay?"

I chewed on my lip and nodded my head.

A woman walked through the door beside Candace's desk. She was older than I expected, probably sixty by my guess. She was dressed in a navy pants suit, and was an attractive woman, but I had little desire to talk to someone that had no idea about what I was going through. I wanted to talk to Candace, she was a survivor. I was done being a victim. I wanted to be a survivor.

"Peyton," Candace said. "This is Elizabeth. She'll take you back where you can talk in private, okay."

"The woman smiled a genuine smile. "Peyton?"

I nodded.

"Hi, I'm Elizabeth. I'm one of the center's counselors, and I'm a survivor," she said.

I felt a little bit better. "Hi, I'm. I'm uhhm. I'm Peyton. Peyton Price."

She extended her hand. I glanced at it, and eventually took her hand in mine.

"Come on back, Peyton," she said. "Who does your hair?"

I reached for my head, and pressed my hair to my scalp. It seemed like an odd question. "My hair?"

"The highlights look wonderful. And I just love the cut. I need to go somewhere new. Mine always looks awful," she said with a laugh.

"Uhhm. The highlights are natural. I spend a lot of time in the sun. I surf. And, thank you. I get it cut at Crystals in Old Town."

I followed her through the door and down a long corridor.

"Crystals?" she asked. "I'll have to give them a try. Who's your stylist?"

"Beth."

"I'll remember that."

She walked through a doorway and into an office. "Have a seat."

The office wasn't like a normal office; it was more like a lounge. I glanced around, sat on an overstuffed chair, and she sat beside me on the edge of a loveseat.

"We have a little different approach here at SDTT. How'd you find out about us?"

I looked around the room. "Google."

"Isn't the internet a wonderful tool?"

I nodded. "Uh huh."

"If I told you I knew how you were feeling would you believe me?"

"Uhhm. Like *really* believe you?"

She laughed. "Yes."

"Probably not."

"I see. Well..." She adjusted herself on the cushion, crossed her legs, and fixed her eyes on mine.

It was the first time I had really noticed her eyes, but they were a lot like Navarro's. A memorizing blue, and definitely not easy to look away from.

"I was seventeen. My husband was twenty-one, and he was at work. We married much younger back then. We'd been married for two years at the time."

I was shocked. "You got married when you were fifteen?"

"I sure did. He was in the military, and we married immediately after he completed his basic training."

"Wow."

She smiled. "I wanted to be the perfect housewife. I had his dinner ready every night when he got home from work. We lived off-base in a small house – just a one bedroom. We were renting it for $250 a month."

I laughed. "Those days are long gone."

"Isn't that the truth," she said. "Would you like something to drink?"

Her voice was soothing, and I enjoyed listening to her tell her story. Although she was considerably younger, she reminded me of my grandmother, which I found comforting. "No. I'm good for now."

She smiled, rested her hands in her lap, and continued. "So, one day, I had dinner in the oven, and was waiting for my husband to come home. A man knocked at the door, and I answered. Back then, people walked from door to door selling things. Door to door salesmen, that's what they called them. We didn't have the internet, or cell phones, for that matter."

I grinned at the thought of living back in the day, and not having all of the distractions of the modern world. Life would be so much different, for sure.

"He was selling vacuum cleaners. I wanted to tell him we couldn't afford one, but to be really honest, I was interested in seeing what it was capable of. A *Kirby*. That's what they called it. Nothing, he said, could get my house cleaner than a Kirby. I had almost an hour to spare before my husband was to get home, so I agreed to see his demonstration."

"Was it as good as he said?"

She shook her head. "We never got that far. He closed the door, locked it, and then he raped me."

My heart sank. I had no idea that's where she was headed with her story. "I'm so sorry."

She smiled a faint but genuine smile and continued. "I felt guilty. For letting him in, you know. I felt responsible, because I was wearing the skirt that my husband liked so much, and though if I had chosen a pants suit, maybe it wouldn't have happened."

She didn't seem upset at all talking about it, but I felt terribly sorry for her nonetheless. To think of someone doing something like that to an unsuspecting housewife was horrible. I stared back at her, at a complete loss for words.

"Mood swings, fits of anger, anxiety, and periods of having less than zero self-esteem followed. It lasted for years. We were trying to have a child at the time, so, I told my husband I needed to go to the doctor. I went that day and got help. I talked to someone like me, a counselor. And, here I am. I've spent my entire life helping people like you and me."

"Thank you. For everything."

"So, if I told you now that I knew how you were feeling, would you believe me?"

I nodded. "Yes."

"Are you ready to talk, Peyton?"

"Yes, ma'am," I said. "I am."

TWENTY-SEVEN

NICK

She thrust her hip into the door of her Jeep, and swung it closed. I watched as she walked into the shop, a plastic bag dangling from her right fist. She swung it back and forth comically, as if to bring attention to the fact she was carrying it. I hadn't seen her for an entire week and I didn't like it much, but she told me she'd come around as soon a she was able.

By the look on her face, she must have been a little more than able.

Smiling from ear to ear, she continued to walk toward me, the grin all but covering her entire face. Watching her walk was a treat in itself, and I could do it for as long as she would let me.

Her jean shorts, Chuck's, and Jimi Hendrix tee shirt were a reminder of the way things once were.

"Here," she said, tossing the bag toward me.

I wasn't expecting her to throw it, but caught it before it fell to the floor, nonetheless. It wasn't heavy, but it was heavier than I expected. "What's this?"

"Open it."

I opened the bag and removed the box that was inside. Covered in Harley-Davidson wrapping paper, the 12-inch by 12-inch box was perfectly wrapped.

"Did you wrap it?"

"No," she said. "I got some random lady to do it."

I nodded and glanced down at the box.

"Yes, asshole. I wrapped it."

"Oh. It looks nice."

"Open it."

"What is it?"

"It's a fucking gift, you big goon."

She's only been gone for a week, and it seemed in the time that she was away, she'd got her spunk back. Surprised, and feeling like I was feeding off of her playful nature, I tossed the box on the workbench and spun her around by her arm. As soon as I did it, I realized I probably shouldn't have. Her reaction told me otherwise.

She bent over and pointed her ass at me. After a few seconds of hovering there bent over, she stood up.

"I thought you were going to spank me. Fucking tease."

"I was just fucking around."

She brushed her hair away from her face. "Open it."

I peeled the paper away from the box carefully, and placed it aside. After opening one of the flaps to the cardboard box and looking inside, I laughed.

"You know what it is? she asked.

I nodded. "Yep."

"So, you've been aware all along that they existed?"

"Yep."

Her eyes narrowed. "When were you going to tell me?"

I shrugged. "I don't know."

"Dick."

"Excuse me?"

"You're a dick."

I opened the other end of the box. "That's kind of harsh."

"Really?" she snapped back. "Why don't you ride on that steel fender for a few hours and then find out they make a little suction cup seat for it. I fucking swear. I was so mad."

I couldn't do anything but laugh. "Sorry."

"The guy at the shop said it was a one-size-fits-all type affair. Is that right?"

I nodded. "Sure is."

"Asshole."

"Enough with the names, you little fucker. Jesus."

"I just can't believe that you've had me on the back of that thing sitting on a bare fender. And, there's another thing I realized after I was looking at some motorcycles at the dealer."

"What's that?"

"You turned it into a hardtail. It doesn't even have fucking shocks."

I chuckled. "Yep."

"Yep it does, or yep it doesn't?"

"It's a hardtail."

"Fucker," she hissed.

"Thanks for the gift, *reporter*."

"You're welcome, *outlaw*."

She looked remarkable. The way she was acting led me to believe she was feeling better about everything. I had no way of knowing if the deaths of the four men contributed to her state of mind, but I really couldn't ask, either. The newspaper had their names listed in the obituaries, but other than that there was nothing on the news, in the newspaper, or on the internet.

Further proof that their lives, in the grand scheme of things, didn't really matter.

"Why are you so fucking giddy today, Peyton?"

She shrugged. "Dunno. Just happy. Maybe it's the seat."

"Quite a bit of excitement over a little seat."

"That little seat's going to make a *huge* difference. That's what the guy said."

The thought of having her on the back of my bike excited me. Especially as happy as she was. "Only one way to find out. Have dinner yet?"

"Not yet, why?"

I tossed her seat in the air. She caught it and grinned.

"Let's roll, reporter."

"Music to my ears, asshole," she snapped back.

And hearing her smart-assed remarks were music to mine.

TWENTY-EIGHT

PEYTON

Two weeks and five sessions of EMDR therapy later, and I was feeling better than I ever believed could have been possible. One eighty-dollar suction cup seat later, and my ass was in heaven. I felt like kidney-punching Navarro as he leisurely rolled down the street for keeping me in the dark about the possibility of a comfortable ride.

We rode along Mission Beach Boulevard after our fish taco dinner, and the ride was a completely different experience altogether. The new seat made riding much more pleasurable. I thought I liked it before, but riding without having my teeth jarred with each bump was allowing me to enjoy everything around us.

I peered beyond the boardwalk and fixed my eyes on the beach. It was late in the evening, and although the sun wasn't setting yet, the low clouds on the horizon seemed to be reaching for the orange ball of fire as it descended toward the ocean.

Seeing the beach, ocean, and soon to be setting sun while riding on my new seat took me to a place I hadn't been since I was a little girl. I tapped Navarro on the shoulder and leaned forward. "Can you pull over?"

"We'll hit Belmont," he said.

"Okay."

HARD

After a few more wonderful minutes of riding, he turned into Belmont Park and came to a stop. I pulled off my helmet, climbed off the bike, and waited for him to get off. Instead of hopping off in a rush like he normally did, he gazed toward the beach for a moment, and then looked right at me.

"Got any plans tonight?"

I hung my helmet on the handlebars and shook my head. "No, why?"

"Want to just sit here and watch the sunset?"

It seemed like an odd question, coming from Navarro. I had hoped that he'd pull over and allow me a few minutes to sit and watch the clouds transform from white marshmallow puffs to picturesque brush strokes of oranges and pinks as they encompassed the sun.

Actually witnessing the sunset, especially with him, seemed like a dream come true.

"I'd love to," I said.

He hung his helmet on the handlebars. I waited for his usual five-steps-ahead *I'm bigger and badder than you* stroll, but he stepped to my right side and waited.

"You ready?" he asked.

I took advantage of the situation, and of him. I gripped his left arm in hand and prepared for his refusal. His eyes met mine, then he looked ahead like nothing had happened. After a few steps, I felt guilty, and released his arm. I really wanted to know if he was going to tell me to get the fuck off of him or if he'd somehow manage to find a way to allow me to touch him.

Knowing he wasn't going to browbeat me over it was nice.

After a few steps, he reached for my wrist, tucked my arm inside of his, and continued walking. No eye contact, no spoken words, just a gentle gesture by a man who probably didn't have a gentle bone in his body.

I fought against my urge to grin, not wanting him to know just how special he was making me feel. I realized we were nothing more than associates, but having someone understand exactly when to act like a human wasn't a common occurrence in the world any longer, and I knew it.

I accepted his offer of kindness and wore an internal smile all the way to Oceanfront Walk. A thigh-high concrete wall separated the walkway from the beach, and when we reached it, we both naturally stopped.

I wondered if he planned on standing there or actually going down to the beach. About the time I decided to ask, he turned to face me.

"You gonna step over that fucker, or you want me to toss you over it?"

I spread my feet shoulder width apart, and gave him my best fighting stance pose. "If you think you're big enough."

For that fleeting moment, I had forgotten that he possessed the skills of a ninja. He reminded me really quick of it, though.

In one effortless move, he picked me up and flipped me over his shoulder and onto the other side of the wall. Somehow, while doing so, he retained control, and lowered me to the ground on the other side.

More than likely some instructional judo move he learned in preparation for combat. No matter how he came to learn it, I was impressed. With him on one side of the wall and me now on the other, I stood there and grinned.

"More soldier bullshit?"

"Soldier?" he snapped. His eyes quickly thinned to slits.

Oh fuck, I hit a nerve.

HARD

I prepared for an evening-ending argument.

"Soldier? For fucks sake. You think I was a *soldier*?"

Not now, no.

He wasn't just acting like he was insulted, he *was* insulted. I didn't know what else to do, so I shrugged.

"United States Navy. SEAL Team One. I wasn't a fucking ground pounder," he barked.

My throat constricted, my mouth went dry, and my pussy started tingling. All at the same time.

I swallowed hard. "You were a SEAL?"

He inhaled a deep breath and glared. After a forced sigh, he shook his head. "Some fucking reporter you are."

He hopped over the wall. "Come on, shit-for-brains, let's go watch the sunset."

We walked down to within a few feet of where the ocean met the land and sat down. The sound of the waves washing ashore was calming, and exactly what I needed. One benefit of having an outlaw biker accompany me to the beach was that most people – upon seeing his kutte and tattoos – decided to move further away, leaving us with our own little private spot.

"Thank you."

He shot me a look. "For what?"

"This."

He shrugged. "Used to do this when I was a kid. We didn't live very far from the beach. It's nice thinking back to when I was a kid. Before things went to shit."

I wondered just what he meant by *before things went to shit*. Eventually, curiosity won the battle, and I proceeded to offer him an even trade. My *when things went to shit* in trade for his.

"When I was eight, my mother went to get some things from the store. My two brothers and I were at school. There was a pileup on the freeway, and she was sitting there waiting on traffic. They said the guy was going seventy or so when he hit the car behind her."

He touched my hand. I looked right at him, and he looked back. We shared a moment with our eyes locked, and then I continued.

"She didn't make it home. They said she wasn't in pain though. I guess it broke her neck. At least that's what they told us. That was when things went to shit for me."

He decided to sit down, and pulled against my wrist as he lowered himself to the sand. We sat side by side with his hand touching my wrist lightly. Just enough that I knew it was there, but I didn't look.

He stared out at the ocean for some time. All the while, he seemed to be doing breathing exercises. In through the nose and out through the mouth, which I never really noticed before. The sound of it became comforting, so instead of disturbing him, I just decided to watch the clouds change color.

"She looked about your age." His eyes were fixed on the beach. "That's what I told myself when I saw her. Twenty-five. I remember thinking that."

If it took him fifteen minutes to develop the courage to speak, I knew better than to look at him. I simply nodded and continued to watch the clouds transform into a rainbow of colors.

"We'd just cleared a building that was filled with insurgents. They were assembling the IED's that were blowing up our troops. A bomb making facility. I stepped around the corner, and there she was. Our eyes locked. She looked worried there for a second, and I figured she was just scared. Hell, everyone was scared. She must have seen it in my eyes. The relaxation, or the tension leaving. I don't know. But she saw *something*."

He turned his head away from me and I heard him spit. He looked back at the horizon, but I didn't turn toward him, I could see him out of my peripheral.

"Whatever she saw let her know I was no longer a threat. She relaxed. I relaxed. We pressed on. Maybe ten meters. And then I saw it. She started to raise a Kalashnikov. It wasn't a choice. It was a combination of training and experience."

He didn't have to say it. My heart sank for him. I lifted my hand and placed it on top of his.

Our hands touched, and he looked at me. The skin under his eyes was swollen, but he wasn't crying. More than anything else, he seemed exhausted. "She was twelve."

He must have seen it in my eyes.

The shock.

I didn't respond.

He looked out at the horizon. "I shot a twelve-year-old girl. You want to know the sad thing?"

I fought to swallow, and once again, didn't respond. The silence encouraged him enough to continue. Either that, or he simply needed to say it.

"If I hadn't shot her, she would have shot me or one of my team members. If I had to do it all over again, I'd do it the same way. Sad, but it's true."

"I'm sorry," I somehow managed to say.

I squeezed his hand for sincerity's sake.

"So, I came home from the war. I'd been fighting in one place or another for fifteen fucking years, and I was ready to settle down. I tried to get a VA loan for a house." He turned toward me and shook his head.

"They denied me. The motherfuckers put me in a position where I had to kill a fucking pre-teen girl, then denied my government home loan because I had insufficient credit. Tell me how the fuck I was supposed to get credit when I was busy fighting for this country's fucking freedom?"

I'm so sorry.

"Anyway. That's when things went to shit for me."

He looked away, obviously upset, but not angry. I was upset too, with our government. I turned toward the setting sun, but left my hand on top of his. He didn't object. Not in the least.

In a few moments, the sky illuminated. It was a glorious display of the most magnificent colors I had ever seen. Slowly, the sun lowered itself into the water.

Together, Navarro and I watched it happen. While we held hands.

On the beach.

TWENTY-NINE

NICK

"My vote's for pork. Beef gets all fucking tough and stringy if you don't do it up right," Pee Bee said.

I turned away from the meat case and shot him a look. "If you don't *do it up right*?"

He nodded. "You know, if a fucker don't know how to cook it."

"What can I get for you?" the butcher asked.

"We're not sure yet," I said. "Give us a minute."

He wiped his hands against his apron and grinned. "I'll be back to check on you in a few minutes."

I turned toward Pee bee. "You come to last year's barbeque, Peeb?"

"You know I did, why?"

"Year before?"

"What the fuck you gettin' at, asshole?"

"Were you here year before last? At the barbeque?"

He sighed, and then nodded. "Yep."

"Was the barbeque good?"

"Damn good."

"Flavorful?"

"It was good as fuck, why?"

"Was any of it stringy or tough?"

HARD

He shook his head. "I just said it was good."

"Ryder was in charge of the smoker for the last two years. If you liked it, it'd stand to fuckin' reason that he'd know how to cook the fuckin' meat."

He shrugged. "Okay."

"We'll get some of each. Fifty-fifty."

"Get more pork than beef. Beef ribs are a fuckin' bitch to get right, Boss."

I folded my arms in front of my chest and glared at him. "Didn't we just settle this? Fifty-fifty?"

"*We* didn't settle it. *You* did. You don't ever fuckin' listen to me. You might ask, but you don't give a fuck what I say."

"Oh, so now you got your fuckin' feelers hurt huh? Over some beef ribs?"

"Make a decision yet? The butcher asked.

We both glared at him.

"I'll just…I'll…I'll come back in a few minutes," he said.

I turned toward Peeb and huffed out a sigh. "You don't pay attention to the details, asshole. I asked you what you liked, not what you wanted. I was being polite. Courteous."

He laughed. "Now you're a kind-hearted fucker, huh?"

"Something like that."

"So you were just askin', but not givin' a fuck what I responded?"

"Jesus fucking Christ. Not exactly. Are we really standing here in the fucking store arguing about meat? Why does everything have to be so god damned difficult with you?"

He shook his head. "It ain't difficult. I ain't difficult. Beef ribs are a bitch to get right. Get pork. That's pretty simple. You wanna be a prick and go fifty-fifty, do it."

I flexed my biceps. "You calling me a prick?"

"I just called you one, yeah. You flexin' on me, Boss?"

I shook my head. "Just asking a question, you big dumb fuck."

"I'll beat your presidential patch-wearin' ass, Crip. Don't call me a dumb fuck."

"Dumb pork-eatin' fuck."

He raked his hair from his face and took a step back. "I mean it."

"So, did you make a decision?" the butcher asked.

We both turned toward him.

His eyes widened. "I'll be back."

"Beef," Pee Bee snapped.

"Pork," I said.

His eyes darted back and forth, alternating between Peeb and me. "Go with a little of each?"

"Fifty-fifty," I said. "We need about 75 pounds of ribs, total. No, make it 80. And 30 pounds of beef brisket."

"When would you like it?"

"Can we pick it up Friday?"

He nodded. "We'll need you to pay in advance on that much meat."

I reached for my wallet. "Just give me an amount."

"So, 40 pounds of beef ribs, 40 pounds of pork ribs, and 30 pounds of beef brisket?"

I nodded. "Sounds right."

He punched his finger against the keyboard on the scale, printed off three stickers, and stuck them to a piece of butcher paper. He handed me the slip of paper. "Just pay at the register. They'll scan those for you."

"Appreciate it."

HARD

He chuckled. "I thought for a minute you two were going to actually fight over it."

"Like a fist fight?" I asked.

He nodded. "That's what I was thinking."

I wagged my finger between Peeb and me. "Who do you think would win?"

The look on his face changed to worried. "Oh, I'd hate to guess."

"Guess." I said.

"I really…"

I narrowed my eyes. "Guess."

He pointed to me.

"Come on, Peeb," I said with a laugh.

"Are you fuckin' kiddin' me?" Pee Bee said, laughing as he spoke. "I've got fifty pounds and seven inches on him. You picked *him*?"

The butcher shrugged.

Pee Bee chuckled. "Why?"

"Why'd I pick him?"

"Yeah, why?"

"Because he looks mean."

"He might look mean, but I *am* mean."

"Come on, tough guy," I said. "Let's go before you hurt someone."

We paid for the meat, and walked out to our bikes.

"Wanna eat?" I asked.

"Sooner or later, yeah."

I raised my leg over the seat and sat down. After strapping on my helmet, I turned toward Peeb. His helmet still hung from his handlebars. He sat staring blankly out at the street.

I cleared my throat. "You coming?"

He nodded. "You bringing her to the barbeque?"

The annual barbeque was a family event and everyone was welcome. "Was thinking about it."

"Funny how things change."

"What do you mean?" I asked.

He looked at me. "You ain't brought anybody to the barbeque since we been havin' 'em. Just funny. Not funny haha, but funny weird."

I glared back at him in disbelief. "It's *weird* that I'm bringing her?"

"Now you're bringing her? Not thinking about it?"

"I'm fuckin' bringing her. Jesus." I shifted my eyes to the street. After a short pause, I continued. "She's a good woman."

"No argument here. It's just weird, that's all."

"Don't make it into something it isn't. She's not my Ol' Lady."

"Ain't makin' it into nothin', Boss. Don't get me wrong, I like that little bitch. A lot. She's good people."

I nodded in agreement. "Fish tacos?"

"Sounds good," he responded. "But changing the subject ain't gonna make me stop asking questions."

He could ask all the questions he wanted, but I was afraid I wouldn't be able to answer them.

Because I had no earthly fucking idea where my life with Peyton was headed.

THIRTY

PEYTON

The night was almost over. Eating barbeque wasn't something I had much experience with, but so far I was enjoying it. At least until the argument started. With Navarro on my left, and Pee bee seated across from me, I felt like I was being attacked from two different directions.

"Just take a bite out of each one and tell us which one's better," Navarro said.

"Hold on a fuckin' minute. Not which one is better," Pee Bee said. "Which one feels better in your mouth. You know, texture or whatever."

"Overall," Navarro said.

"Yeah. What he said. Taste, *texture*, and if the meat's all stringy and kinda nasty or tough to eat, don't be afraid to say so."

"Just stop," I shouted. "You two are like a couple of little kids. Hold on."

They looked the same to me, and I had no idea why they were having me sample ribs. Eating meat off a bone was pretty gross in my opinion, no matter what it was. For the sake of ending their argument, however, I agreed to give it a try.

I bit some of the meat off the rib on the left, chewed it, and swallowed it. It was kind of greasy, but it tasted good. The right rib followed, and the meat wasn't as easy to chew, but it had great flavor.

HARD

I wiped my fingers on the napkin. There was no way to pick. Both were equally gross. I did *eeny, meeny, miny, moe* and picked up the rib on the right. Pee Bee's eyes went wide and he smiled from ear to ear.

It wasn't what I wanted.

I waved the rib in the air. "This one sucked ass."

Pee Bee's hand slapped the table. "Fuck!"

"Told you," Navarro said. He held out his hand. "Pay up, sucka!"

Pee Bee dug in his wallet, and then handed him a $20 bill. "Fuck off. She's not a rib expert."

Navarro put the money in his pocket. "She sure picked it."

Pee Bee glared at me. "Fuckin' novice."

I shrugged.

He got up and walked away, leaving Navarro and me sitting alone. Most of the other people were walking around, dancing, or just standing and talking. It was nice to meet more of Navarro's group. Seeing the men with their girlfriends, wives, or whoever they chose to bring was nice.

"Here, I'll toss that in the trash for you."

"Thanks," I said.

He took my plate and walked toward the trash can, which was up by the building. While he was walking back to the table, two guys stopped him to talk. Five minutes later, when he hadn't returned, I glanced nervously around the packed parking lot.

Men in vests were everywhere, but it wasn't solely FFMC's men. Various other members of clubs were scattered about, talking to each other or just standing and drinking beers alone. I was seated at a group of picnic style tables, and as most people were walking around drinking, I was left sitting alone.

I am in control.

I am safe now.

I looked toward the building, and saw Navarro trying to make his way back to the table. After waving off a few men who tried to get him to talk, he finally sat down beside me at the table.

"Tell me the truth?"

"I'm bound by a promise, remember?"

He chuckled. "Oh, yeah."

"What's the question?"

"The rib. The one you picked up. Were you going to say that it was the good one, and then you changed your mind when you saw Peeb celebrating?"

I nodded. "Yep."

"No shit?"

"No shit."

"You didn't like the other one?"

"It was kinda weird. They were both gross, but the other one was more gross."

He twisted his mouth to the side. "Fuck."

"Fuck what?"

"I'm going to have to give him his money back."

I shrugged. "Maybe wait till tomorrow. It'd be more fun."

"I'll probably do that."

"Thanks, by the way. I don't remember if I told you that. But thanks."

"For?"

"Letting me come."

"I didn't let you come," he said. "I asked you to come. There's a difference."

It seemed like splitting hairs to me. "Thanks for *asking* me to come."

He grinned, but I was left wondering what he meant by what he said. It gnawed on me for a minute, and then I asked.

"What's the difference? Between letting me and asking me?"

"Letting you would be agreeing to allow you to come if you asked if you could. If you said, *hey can I come to your barbeque?* Asking you to come means I wanted you to come, and I asked you, because I wanted you here."

I liked the difference that he explained, but I wanted to know more. There was no way that Navarro and I would ever amount to anything more than elbow-rubbing associates, but it was nice to dream.

Now that I knew him better, I found him to be so much more than an intriguing biker. He was caring, could be kind, and most of what others saw in him was a hard outer layer that he used to protect his significantly more sensitive inner being.

Getting through the outer shell wasn't easy, though.

"Why'd you ask me? Or why'd you want me?"

His response was quick and without thought or hesitation.

"I like you," he said.

It wasn't much.

In fact, I'd been told a lot more than that from lesser men over the years. But, coming from Navarro, it was pretty fucking significant.

At least to me.

The sound of the people, the music, and even what I could see of my surroundings all became insignificant. Elizabeth told me to always be aware of my surroundings, but at that moment I wasn't.

And it didn't matter.

I had tunnel vision, and all I could see was Navarro.

I leaned forward. It was a long shot, but it was worth a try.

He leaned into me, and kissed me lightly on the lips.

"I'm not broken," I said. "Really."

He wrapped his hand around the back of my neck, pulled me into him, and kissed me like I had never been kissed.

Ever.

My mind raced. His beard against my face reminded me that he was a real man, and I liked it.

Both of my palms went sweaty and I wiped them on my shirt. Passion filled me from head to toe, and a tingling shot through me, shaking me to my core. Our tongues intertwined and we fought to find the perfect spot for our hands to land, but it seemed to never happen.

While we continued to grope and kiss, Pee Bee's complaint brought us both back to the reality of the situation.

"Get a fuckin' room, Crip!"

Our mouths parted. I looked at him.

He looked back at me.

He stood and reached for my hand.

"What?" I asked.

"Come on," he said.

The party wasn't over, and I knew he really didn't want to go anywhere. I loved kissing him, but making out in the shop on the bench would just ruin it for me.

"Where are we going?"

"To my house," he said. "We need to be laying on *something squishy*."

Something squishy.

I like that.

THIRTY-ONE

NICK

I had sex for one reason, and one reason only. To blow my load. I had never been concerned with a woman's desires, needs, or thoughts. Now, Peyton's desires, needs, and thoughts were *all* I was concerned with.

My hands pressed against the soft skin of her breasts. I waited for rejection, but received none. Carefully, I kneaded her flesh, paying special attention not to be too rough. She wiggled and twisted her body, but I could tell by her moans that she was as pleased as I was.

I lowered my mouth to meet her nipples, kissing them softly with my lips, then following with a few flicks of my tongue. She responded by digging her nails into my back, further proof that so far I had yet to make a mistake.

Perfection wasn't my goal, nor was it an expectation. I wanted to please her, and the thought of doing so pleased me. It was a first, that was for sure.

Before the barbeque, I had an idea of how I felt about Peyton, but I wasn't certain what I wanted in the end. When we kissed, something either changed, or I came to a realization. As ridiculous as it seemed to admit afterward, kissing her was all the confirmation my mind needed.

With my body, spirit, and soul released from my mind's grip, I cautiously worked to satisfy her, hoping to bring her to climax without causing her any mental or physical pain.

I sucked and kissed her breasts repeatedly, grinding my hips against hers with each touch of my lips to her nipples.

Her moaning continued, and fueled by her expressed pleasure, I continued.

Several minutes later, the moaning had all but stopped.

She pressed her elbows into the mattress and lifted her head. "Uhhm. I'm more than a set of nice tits. You know that, right?"

"Huh?"

"You've been fucking around with my tits since we started," she complained. "I told you, I'm not broken."

Hurting her in any way would crush me. Still harboring the guilt for what happened to her, an extremely cautious advance was all she was going to receive from me. At least for now. "I know," I said. "But I just don't want to--"

She flipped her hair over her shoulder. "Hurt me?"

I nodded. "Yeah."

She sat up completely. "I'm safe with you. That's one thing I need to always remind myself of, and I do. I'm safe here."

I rolled to the side and continued to listen, but paid more attention to admiring her perfect body.

"You're not going to hurt me," she said. "We both know it. Ultimately, I'm in control. Me. Not you. Me."

"Okay."

"I'm safe, and I'm in control. But guess what?"

I was lost. Completely. "What?"

"I want you to fuck me. And I don't mean I want you to stick your cock in me and gently work your hips back and forth. If we're going to do this, I want to be *fucked*."

"I just...I don't want to--"

"Hurt me? Roll over," she said. "I fucking swear. If a woman want's something done right, she's got to do it herself."

THIRTY-TWO

PEYTON

On his back with his raging cock pointing at the sky, Navarro looked at me with guilt in his eyes. I wrapped my hands around his thick shaft and looked him in the eye. "Watch me. Okay?"

His Adam's apple rose and then fell. "Okay."

I worked his cock in and out of my mouth until it was deep in my throat. After the tip caused me to gag a few times, I raised my head and met his gaze.

With wide eyes, he looked back at me.

I wiped my mouth on the back of my hand. "See, I'm fine."

"Uh huh," he murmured.

I considered sucking his cock for a few more minutes, but I didn't ponder it for long. The aching in my pussy was more than I could stand. As a result of him sucking my tits into a frenzy and me gratefully gagging on his thick cock, I was more than ready to feel him deep inside of me.

I straddled him and studied his muscled torso. Covered in tattoos and not wearing a shirt, he looked ten times better than he did with one on, that was for sure. I licked my lips at the sight of his chiseled abs.

"Grab my waist," I said.

He placed his hands against my hips.

"No," I said with a laugh. I raised his hands to my waist. "Here. My waist."

I gripped his cock in my hand, hovered over him, and then guided him into me. Although the first attempt didn't go very deep, feeling him inside of me sucked the air from my lungs. I gulped a breath, raised myself up and then forced him into my drenched pussy again.

And again.

Then, taking his full length, I began to ride his cock like it was the last cock on earth.

I slapped my hands against his chest. "Fuck yes. See? You. Feel. Fucking. Amazing. God, I needed this."

I thrust my hips back and forth, taking every inch of him in with each downward motion.

"Grab my tits," I said. "Squeeze 'em."

As I continued to fuck him like a woman on some kind of a once-in-a-lifetime sexual mission, he began to squeeze and suck my boobs.

His mood soon changed from the overcautious protector to bad-ass biker, and it was exactly what I needed. While nibbling on my tits, he bit into one of my nipples. *Hard.* I wailed out from the extreme mixture of pleasure from the pain.

"Ouch!"

His eyes shot wide, and he pulled away.

"Do it again," I gasped. "Bite me."

He sank his teeth into my nipples gently and eventually began to bite them. I closed my eyes and continued to fuck him with all I had. As the bed creaked from my frantic thrusts, my breathing became irregular, and I felt somewhat embarrassed.

I was reaching climax, and he wasn't.

I tried my best to hide my pleasure, hoping to slip an orgasm past him without his knowledge. As my emotions began to mount, I closed my eyes and allowed the orgasm to shoot through me like an electric shock.

I shook from head to toe, and the pace of my strokes slowed considerably.

Exhausted and feeling rather sensitive in the downtown region, I climbed from his cock and bought myself a moment's time.

I stroked his cock a few times, then began to suck it like I was in a timed event, trying to beat the clock. His hips began to lift from the bed slightly, and when I realized it, I raised my mouth from the tip and fought to catch my breath.

"Fuck my mouth."

"What?"

"Fuck. My. Mouth."

"Get on your knees."

I complied. He got off the bed and stood in front of me with his thick cock sticking straight out, he gripped my head in his hands, and began to shove his cock down my throat.

"That's right, suck that cock," he growled.

Oh, God yes.

Talk dirty to me.

He forced himself deep into my throat, causing my eyes to water from the force. "I'm going to make you gag on this motherfucker if it's the last thing I do."

After a few seconds my eyes began to bulge, and I slapped my hand against his thigh, tapping out.

He pulled himself from my mouth, and immediately after I gasped a breath, he forced himself right back into my throat.

"You're a good little bitch," he growled. "Now suck that cock like you know you can."

He rocked back and forth on the balls of his feet, forcing the tip of his dick into to the soft flesh in my throat. I reached down and fingered my clit as the shaft of his cock stretched my mouth wide. Nick's trusting that I was not broken was bringing me dangerously close to another orgasm. I pulled myself away and fought to catch a breath. As I gasped for air, he lifted me from the floor by my arms.

"Bend over," he said.

Fuck yes.

I bent over the end of the bed and hiked my ass high in the air. I was soaked and more than ready for whatever he had to offer.

He seized me from behind, slid in with ease, and began to fuck me deeply. In no time, he had my hair in his hand, his muscular chest pressed into my back, and his mouth on my right ear.

"I'm going to fill your tight little pussy with cum," he breathed.

Oh God.

"Full," he said.

Please...

My body began to tingle.

I spread my feet wider. His balls began tapping a tune on my clit with each stroke. I bit into my lower lip, prepared for the orgasm of the century, and waited.

A few strokes later, and my eyes went wide. I felt like I was on the verge of coming apart. I wanted to scream for him to stop, fearing something was wrong, but before I had a chance to throw in the towel, I exploded.

"Ohmyfuckinggod!" I stammered. "Ohmyfuckinggod!"

I must have repeated myself half a dozen times as the jolts ran through me like mini-lightning bolts.

His cock swelled, and he pulled my hair taught. "Fuck yes!" he wailed. "Here I come!"

His breath went from grunts against my neck and face to irregular fits of breathing that burst out into the open room.

And he came.

Another orgasm shot through me as I felt him discharge into my cervix. I cried out in pleasure, gripped the comforter tight in my hands, and came close to crying from the pleasure I felt.

Seconds later we had collapsed side-by-side on the bed, our legs dangling over the edge, and our arms draped to the sides.

He turned to the side and gripped my neck in his hand. I sighed and met his gaze as he pulled against my neck, forcing my lips to his. A few kisses later, and he pulled away and looked me in the eye.

"My little bitch," he said.

Hearing that wouldn't have made very many women happy, but I wasn't very many women.

"I sure am."

THIRTY-THREE

NICK

I couldn't claim to have fallen in love before, so identifying what it was I felt and giving it a label wasn't something I found easy to do. And, to be truthful, with me being a big bad-ass biker, even if I was in love, I probably wouldn't want to admit it.

But I was able to identify pride.

And I was proud of having Peyton in my life.

I turned the corner and rolled up the street. Not in a million lifetimes would I have guessed I'd be doing what I was doing.

"Why won't you just tell me?" she asked.

"Because it's a surprise."

"I think that's chicken-shit," she said.

I released the throttle and coasted down the street. "See the light blue one over there?"

She leaned forward and rested her chin on my shoulder. "The one with the big rock garden?"

"Yep."

"What about it?"

"Brent Houseman lived there. We were buddies in high school."

"You used to live around here?"

"Yep."

"Cool"

The bike slowed to an almost stop, but I had half a block or so to go, so I rolled on a little throttle. "The yellow one over there was where Becky Tharp lived. She was a cheerleader. And, no, I didn't bang her. She was a bitch."

"Nice to know," she said.

As we came closer, I felt nervous, and really, nothing made me nervous. Hell, I had walked into abandoned buildings that were filled with men who were armed and wanted to kill me, and I wasn't as nervous as I was with her.

"See the white one there on the right?"

"Yep."

"That's where I grew up."

Her grip on my waist tightened, and she leaned forward. "Really?"

"Yep."

"Until when? When did you move out?"

I shifted into neutral and rolled to a stop in the middle of the street, thirty feet or so from the drive. The exhaust rumbled a low drone as it idled, echoing the sound of our arrival for all to hear.

"When I went to war, pretty much."

"Oh wow. Where do your parents live now?"

I motioned toward the house. "Still live right there."

"You're not. Were you. Is that where we're going?"

"Yep. If you're ready, that is."

"Nick, you shit-head. Really?"

"If you're ready. If you're not, tell me now so I can get the fuck out of here before either of them see me."

"I'm wearing shorts, Chuck's and a shitty shirt," she complained.

"You look cute," I assured her. "Yes, or no?"

"I mean, I want to, but--"

"Yes, or no?"

"I would love to, but I look like--"

I pulled in the clutch, shifted into gear, and released it. As the bike got even with the drive, she slapped my shoulder.

"Yes."

I got on the brakes, but it was too late. I rolled past and had to turn around in the middle of the street to get into the drive.

We parked, and I shut off the bike. "Ready?"

"Oh boy." She took off her helmet, brushed the wrinkles from her shirt, and adjusted her ponytail. "Okay."

I hung my helmet on the bars. "Let's do it."

Together we nervously walked up the walk. After stepping on the porch, I rapped my knuckles against the door three times.

"Enter!"

And I opened the door.

THIRTY-FOUR

PEYTON

Nick opened the door and I stepped inside. I hadn't seen my father since Christmas. After his relocation to North Carolina, the holidays were the only time I saw him or my brothers. I hoped meeting Nick's mother and father, although traumatic, would provide me comfort.

I stepped to Nick's side. He rested his left arm on my shoulder, and sighed. "Pop, this is Peyton."

His father jumped from the chair he was sitting in and held out his right hand. He looked just like Nick, only twenty or so years older. Regardless of his age, I was shocked at the similarities in their appearance. "Well shit, Son. You should have warned us. Nice to meet you, Peyton."

"We were just in the neighborhood," Nick said. "Thought we'd stop by for a minute."

I heard some noise in the kitchen, and suspected it was his mother.

"Our son's here!" his father yelled. "And he brought a surprise."

I laughed to myself at the fact he yelled at her like she was a mile away, when in fact she was only a few feet away.

"We'll go in there," Nick said. "Be right back."

I followed him to the kitchen. When we stepped in, his mother was at the sink, bent over scrubbing it with a scouring pad.

HARD

"Always doing something," he said. "Turn around, I want you to meet someone."

She sighed, and turned around.

Oh my God.

I almost fainted. My legs went wobbly. I may have even gasped, but I wasn't sure. If I did, no one said anything afterward. I fought to stay composed, and although it wasn't easy, I followed her lead.

"Well, aren't you a sight for sore eyes?" She wiped her hands on her apron. "I'm Elizabeth, Nicholas' mother. What was your name?"

I swallowed heavily and fought not to cry. "Peyton," I said. "Peyton Price."

But she already knew my name. She was the woman who saved me from myself.

"It's so nice to meet you, Peyton," she said. "Nicholas, go take off that thing, and come back when it's gone."

Nick sighed. "Fine. I'll hang it on my bike."

He walked away. I stood there, not knowing what to do or say. She gripped my hand in hers, pulled me to her side, and rinsed the sink. "It's so nice to have you here."

She knew everything about me. I'd told her about the incident entirely, about my mother dying, and about all of my quirks, shortcomings, and my strengths. I'd told her about my job, the need to write the article, and about having a man in my life that I wasn't sure about.

I had, more than anything, simply told her the truth. Knowing that she knew everything about me, I couldn't help but wonder if she would accept me or reject me as Nick's significant other.

"Thank you," I said.

"Do you know how to make chicken marsala?" she asked.

I shook my head. I really didn't know how to make much. Growing up without a mother, going to college, and having a demanding job left me with little time to learn to cook.

"No," I said.

She took me by the hand and led me to the oven. "Stand right there, and let me get everything. We'll make it together, how's that?"

I grinned. "Sounds good."

"*Sounds good?*" She chuckled, then opened the refrigerator door. "Nicholas says that all the time, and now he's got you saying it. It's nice to see he's rubbing off on you. He's a nice boy."

I nodded. "He is."

She placed everything on the countertop.

"All he's ever needed was a nice girl." She looked me in the eye, and smiled. "I'm so glad he finally found one."

She wrapped her arms around me and held me tight.

I loved having Nick hold me and hug me, but there would never be anything that would come close to be being held in a mother's arms.

Elizabeth may not have been my mother, but my heart sure didn't know it.

THIRTY-FIVE

PEYTON

I sat at my desk with my fingers hovering over the keyboard, knowing I was on the verge of losing my job.

If it bleeds, it sells.

Words to live by in the world of journalism.

Children being saved from a burning building were never as popular as a mass shooting. A front page color photo of a sunset would sit stagnant, while a front page color photo of a grotesquely graphic car wreck would sell out.

I needed something graphic, something gut-wrenching, something memorable.

But, I refused to use Nick or his club as a vehicle to sell newspapers. There were many stories to tell, but none that I was willing to divulge. Camden Rollins III would probably fire me when it was all over, but I could *not* pen a vicious story about Nick and the FFMC.

At least not something worth reading.

I decided, above all, I needed to write a story that made a difference. Something that was gut-wrenching, but not too gory. A heartfelt, but tear-jerking story that stuck with the reader long after they were done reading it. Something that made them say, *what the fuck was that about?*

Something they may even read again. After they thought about it.

HARD

I relaxed in my chair, stared at my monitor, and sighed. After a long period of silence, it came to me.

My fingers no longer hovered over the keyboard. They tapped at record pace. In a few hours, I had the story.

I read it, re-read it, and printed a copy.

Proudly, I walked into Mr. Rollins' office, tossed it on his desk, and grinned. "Sorry I'm a few months late."

His eyes met mine. After a short glare, he picked it up. A few seconds later, he looked up, but his eyes fell right back down to the page.

When he finished, he dropped it onto his desk.

"This? This is why I let you do what you want, when you want."

I grinned. "Like it?"

He shook his head. "Love it."

"Thank you," I said.

"I'm rolling with this on Sunday. What'll the headline say, Peyton?"

I shrugged. "Call it what it is."

He widened his eyes.

"Hard," I said. "Call it *hard*."

Because it was.

EPILOGUE

NICK

Peyton, Pee Bee, and I were at the shop, trying to decide where to go to lunch.

"It's Sunday," Pee Bee said. "Nothing's fucking open that's good."

"Pizza?" Peyton asked. "Haven't had pizza in forever."

"I'm not interested," I said.

"Shit," Pee Bee said, his voice a few octaves lower than normal.

"What?"

"Behind you," he said. "Your fucking buddy."

I turned around just in time to see the detective pull into the parking lot.

My asshole puckered at the thought of being arrested again, or being questioned in front of Peyton.

His car came to a stop beside us. He rolled his window down, and reached into the passenger seat. After turning around, he stuck his head out the window and grinned. "Can you read, Navarro?"

I nodded. "Comics and shit, yeah?"

He tossed me a newspaper. "Read that," he said. "That right there? The front page? That's good shit."

"Peanut Butter, Navarro, Mrs. Price." He nodded toward each of us as he said our names. "Have a nice day."

HARD

He grinned and drove away.

I opened the paper, saw the headline, and made note of the reporter's name. I looked at Peyton.

She shrugged.

And, I began to read.

***

A mother dies in a horrific car crash, leaving her children to be raised by an overworked father and an immigrant babysitter. No one cares, because there wasn't a photo attached to the story of her death.

A pic or it didn't happen.

If it bleeds, it sells. But that shouldn't be the case. The world has changed. A best-selling love story will soon be a thing of the past. If it hasn't happened yet, it'll be here before you know it. The romance world has been turned on its ear by step-brother romances, slaughterotica, and priests with a penchant for girls.

It must be shocking, or it won't sell. If it's a tale of love, hatred – or anything in between – it doesn't sell. And it won't.

Be the first to pen a new way to have sex with a corpse, and you'll hit the New York Times best-sellers list. Write a book about two people who fall in love, get married, and have triplets, and you'll go broke.

Front page articles are used to sell the newspaper. The cover story. Lure them in at any and all costs. Write it long enough to require them to flip to two or three more pages, and you've done your job.

How does a journalist tell a tale of love and still capture the interest of the reader enough to provoke them to complete the story?

Make it a shocker.

Race. Color. Creed. Religion. In the eyes of the almighty, we're equal and we should remain so, but we don't. As a nation, we've been taught to judge. The world, in fact, has been taught to judge.

We tell ourselves we don't, but we do.

A man at a red light sits quietly with his wife and children, listening to his favorite music. A sound in the distance makes the hair on the back of his neck stand up. He fills with fear, for he has heard the sound before, and he knows what it brings.

"Don't look," he warns the family.

A group of men on motorcycles pull alongside the Buick. The man, petrified, stares straight ahead and prays to his maker for the traffic light to turn green before something happens.

Because something, he is certain, will happen.

The light turns, and he speeds away.

Is he right, or is he wrong?

At a bar the motorcyclists stop. Once inside, they notice a woman. A woman who is alone. One-by-one, they take their turn, raping her. They rape her of her innocence, of her trust, and of her ability to sleep at night. They rape her of her life.

Yet, somehow, she survives.

She stumbles through her days and nights that follow, not knowing how – or even if – she'll ever survive.

The rapists are eventually caught, taken to court, and tried for the horrific crime they committed. After a lengthy trial, they are convicted and await sentencing. On judgment day, they receive six months in the county jail – in protective custody.

Even jailhouse justice is impossible. They're protected from harm.

The girl, once again, is raped.

HARD

By the judicial system.

Downtrodden and beaten, she stumbles to the bar, hoping to dull the pain. Halfway through her first pitcher of beer, she hears a familiar rumble. Through the window, she confirms her suspicions.

A motorcycle club.

In fear for her life, she attempts to grab her things and go. Before she is able, however, they are upon her. Slowly, and without expression, one of the men approaches her. She cowers in her seat. He reaches for her.

She flinches.

And he picks a piece of lint from her coat.

"We heard about your case," he says. "Don't worry. Justice will prevail."

She swallows hard, and attempts to acknowledge his presence, but the words do not come.

He physically looks no different than the men who haunt her dreams, but somehow she feels that he is.

With a glimmer of hope, her eyes meet his. Memorizing and blue, they provide her with comfort.

Embarrassed for her initial fear of the club's intentions, her eyes fall to the floor. When she looks up, the men are gone.

She hears the rumble. Through the window, she watches as the taillights fade off into the darkness of the night, and her heart fills with warmth.

Is she right, or is she wrong?

Six months later, on the eve of their release, the rapists leave their protective cells. One by one, they walk away.

And one by one they meet their fate.

When the woman gets the news, she feels justice is served.

Right, I ask you? Or wrong?

For the first time since that horrific night, she falls into a deep uninterrupted sleep.

And she dreams.

She dreams of equality.

Of love.

And of a world that does not, will not, and cannot hate.

The familiar rumble wakes her from her sleep. Through the window she sees the man, sitting on his motorcycle.

Waiting.

And, without hesitation, she climbs on the back of the motorcycle, and she rides away.

Forever.

Right, or wrong?

Ask her the next time she crosses your path.

She is any survivor.

Signed, a survivor.

Made in the USA
Middletown, DE
24 July 2016